“Have you ever wanted a night to last forever, Jane?”

Adam’s hold on her tightened as they danced, and she was glad that she didn’t have to meet his eyes.

“Yes, once... a long time ago... when I was much younger.”

“Only once?”

She nodded. “What about you?”

“More than once, but not for some time. In fact, not since that night we had dinner in London.”

What did he mean? In the same moment that she glanced up, Adam released her hand, moving his own hand to her face and tilting it upward. Then he bent his head and kissed her.

Anne Weale and her husband live in a Spanish villa high above the Mediterranean. An active woman, Anne enjoys swimming, interior decorating and antique hunting. But most of all, she loves traveling. Researching new romantic backgrounds, she has explored New England, Florida, Canada, Australia, Italy, the Caribbean and the Pacific.

Books by Anne Weale

ANTIGUA KISS
FLORA
SUMMER'S AWAKENING

HARLEQUIN ROMANCE

2484–BED OF ROSES
2940–NEPTUNE'S DAUGHTER
3108–THAI SILK
3132–SEA FEVER
3216–PINK CHAMPAGNE
3257–THE SINGING TREE

HARLEQUIN PRESENTS

846–FRANGIPANI
1013–GIRL IN A GOLDEN BED
1061–NIGHT TRAIN
1085–LOST LAGOON
1133–CATALAN CHRISTMAS
1270–DO YOU REMEMBER BABYLON?

THE FABERGÉ CAT

Anne Weale

Harlequin Books

TORONTO • NEW YORK • LONDON
AMSTERDAM • PARIS • SYDNEY • HAMBURG
STOCKHOLM • ATHENS • TOKYO • MILAN
MADRID • WARSAW • BUDAPEST • AUCKLAND

ISBN 0-373-03318-4

THE FABERGÉ CAT

This edition published by arrangement with Harlequin Enterprises B. V.

Printed in U.S.A.

CHAPTER ONE

'IS THAT you, Jane?'

The elderly voice came from the ground-floor room at the front of what had once been a large family house but now was divided into bed-sitters and small apartments.

Jane Taunton, who was in the act of shaking out her umbrella before closing the front door, felt her heart sink slightly.

She was fond of old Mrs Chichester, the owner of the house, and happy to do her shopping and to spend several evenings a week keeping her company. But it had been a difficult day at the office where Jane was a secretary. Coming home to the old London house, on the north side of Hyde Park, she had some way to walk from the nearest Underground station. Tonight, as she was hurrying back in heavy rain, a taxi had sped through a puddle, splashing water over her legs.

She was longing to run a deep bath and soak her weary bones. They ought not to be weary. She still had three years to go to her thirtieth birthday. But this evening she felt as if fifty was looming ahead of her. She was tired, depressed, sick of city life and an interminably wet winter.

None of these inner feelings showed in her smiling face as she entered the cluttered room where her landlady, once the wife of a leading surgeon, lived among the relics of her prosperous past.

Now in her late eighties, long widowed and still quietly grieving for her sons, both killed in World War II, Mrs Chichester responded to Jane's cheerful enquiry, 'How are you this evening?' by waving a piece of white card.

'I've been asked to a party but you shall go in my place and tell me all about it.' The still bright eyes in the ravaged old face twinkled with excitement and pleasure. 'It's a fortnight on Thursday at Crowthorne's gallery in Brook Street. A private view of an exhibition of paintings..."Two Hundred Years of Beautiful Women". You must wear my Vionnet dress. Who knows? You may meet your fate.'

Jane had no desire to go to a fashionable gathering of the rich and famous where she wouldn't know anyone and would feel totally out of her element. At the same time she didn't wish to cast a damper on Mrs Chichester's enthusiasm for what she evidently saw as a wonderful opportunity for Jane to meet some eligible men.

In the old lady's heyday, meeting and captivating a *parti* had been the main purpose in life of every unmarried 'gel' in her stratum of society. In this, as in other ways, she found it difficult to accept that times had changed.

Even though Mrs Chichester was among the very few people who knew Jane's secret, she still refused to admit that a marriage to a successful and charming man, such as she herself had achieved, was not on the cards for her protégée.

'I should have thought Crowthorne's would have crossed me off their invitation list by now,' Olivia Chichester said wryly. 'I suppose they are hoping I still have some treasures for them to sell. I only wish I had. But the last of my valuable paintings was auctioned five years ago when the roof had to be repaired. I still have a John Smart portrait miniature which might fetch a good price. But I shan't sell that till I'm desperate... or dead,' she added, with a chuckle. 'Let's have a glass of sherry. Take off your wet coat, my dear. How thankful I am that I wasn't born in your generation. Going out to work every day, in all weathers, wouldn't have suited me at all.'

It was nearly an hour before Jane felt able to say good-night and go up to her three-room apartment on the floor above.

Deeply lonely herself, she sympathised with Mrs Chichester's plight, exacerbated in the old lady's case by age and infirmity.

Her spirits lifted a little when she had switched on the lamps and the artificial log fire in the large, high-ceilinged sitting-room which, with very little money to spare, she had done her best to make homely.

Leading off it was a small bedroom with an adjoining bathroom. The garden behind the house went with the flat in the basement. Jane, who longed for a garden, had to make do with boxes on the sills outside her sitting-room windows and a few pots wired, Spanish-fashion, to the cast-iron landing of the fire escape.

To frustrate burglars this stopped well short of the ground and from the lowest landing there was a let-down ladder. Even so, a policeman from the crime prevention squad had advised Mrs Chichester that the fire escape made the windows at the back of the house vulnerable.

Concerned for the safety of her tenants, all of them single women, she had spent money she could ill afford having metal security grilles installed at all the rear windows.

Jane cooked for herself and the old lady most weekends. During the week Mrs Chichester had her main meal at midday, prepared for her by Winnie, a somewhat slapdash but kind-hearted daily help. Jane had a sandwich lunch and usually bought her supper ready-made from a supermarket and heated it in her second-hand microwave oven.

Tonight, instead of having a bath before supper, she stuffed her wet shoes with paper and put them to dry not too close to the fire. Then she changed into a dressing-gown and prepared a small salad before heating a shop-bought lasagne.

While she ate, she re-read the invitation Mrs Chichester had insisted on her bringing upstairs with her.

Like everything connected with Crowthorne's, the famous fine arts auctioneers founded in 1746, the large white card was of superior quality and the black copperplate writing on it was expensively engraved. No doubt Crowthorne's had their own printing works where their gold-embossed royal purple catalogues, many of them collectors' items, were produced.

As she studied the card with its request, in the bottom left-hand corner, to *répondez, s'il vous plaît*, she began to wonder if it might not be fun to accept the invitation.

She so rarely went anywhere. Even though she would be a fish out of water, knowing no one else there and known to none of the grandees, there would be the paintings to admire and no doubt some nice things to eat.

Also it would disappoint Mrs Chichester if she didn't go. The old lady would have liked to go herself but her painful hip and swollen ankles made it impossible for her to stand for more than a few minutes at a time.

And although she had a wardrobe of beautiful 1930s clothes which sometimes she asked Jane to model for her, to revive memories of her happiest days, none of her elegant evening dresses would fit her now that her figure had expanded into a cottage-loaf shape.

If Jane went in her place at least she would be able to describe the occasion in more detail than was likely to be reported in Mrs Chichester's newspaper.

A few days before the private view party, Jane had a letter from her sister Alice who was happily married and lived in the north of England.

As usual Alice's letter was mainly about the children; her twin sons, Angus and Fergus, who would soon be thirteen, Rory aged ten, and eight-year-old Apple who was Jane's god-daughter.

Her sister's life as a country housewife, surrounded by a growing family and sheltered by a kind if slightly dull husband who no longer played rugger himself but spent his Saturdays coaching the Colts team, was the life Jane would have liked, given a choice.

But, as she had discovered, the way things worked out was often a matter of chance rather than choice. So here she was, trapped in a city where she had no wish to be, in a job which did not greatly interest her but paid the rent and her other expenses, with no prospect of changing her circumstances.

Perhaps, when Mrs Chichester died, she would take steps to find a more interesting job outside London. But to go now would leave the old lady without a friend in the world, for she did not care for any of her other tenants and her only relations, a middle-aged nephew and his wife, never came near her.

Alice had written:

> Apple has a bad cold. I'm keeping her in bed for a day or two. She's a good patient, quite content as long as she has a jigsaw puzzle or a book to read. You were the same as a child. I hated being kept indoors and grizzled and groaned as the boys do whenever they're laid up, which isn't often, thank goodness.

The picture of cosy domesticity conjured up by her sister's letter made Jane long to be there, rubbing Vick on Apple's bony little chest, making hot lemon and honey to soothe her cough and reading aloud from the old-fashioned children's books Mrs Chichester had given Jane to send to her; *What Katy Did*, *Little Women* and *Anne of Green Gables*.

Apple was different from the rest of Alice's big-boned, athletic brood. They took after their tall, sturdy parents. Apple was also tall, but like Jane at the same age she was fine-boned and coltish.

Jane spent her lunch-hour in the office, writing a letter to her god-child about the party at Crowthorne's and what she might choose to wear from all the glamorous clothes in Mrs Chichester's wardrobe. Apple adored dressing up.

> Mrs Chichester wants me to wear a black velvet dress by a French designer, Madeleine Vionnet, who was the first person to cut materials on the cross to make them hang in a more fluid way than before. But there's also a lovely dress by Molyneux which might be more suitable. I'm going to have my hair specially done.

Even at the place around the corner a shampoo and set is very expensive. So Winnie's daughter, Anita, is doing it for me. She's an apprentice at a very grand hairdresser's in Mayfair where princesses and film stars go. At the moment Anita is only allowed to sweep up cut hair and make coffee for the clients, but Winnie says she has picked up a lot of expertise just by watching the stylists.

'You look ravishing, my dear,' said Mrs Chichester, when Jane was ready to set out. 'Anita has done your hair beautifully and that dress looks wonderful on you. No one would ever guess it was more than fifty years old, except that silk velvet of that exquisite quality is probably not made today, even for the French *haute couture* houses.'

Jane looked at her reflection in the cheval-glass in the old lady's bedroom. Winnie and Anita were also there, their dark faces smiling approval.

Winnie, whose parents had come to England from the Caribbean, had inherited their way of speaking, but Anita was all young Londoner with a Cockney accent she was trying to change to the 'posh' voice used by the stylists when talking to clients, if not always behind the scenes.

'You shoulda been a model, not a secretary, Jane,' she said, pleased with her success at transforming Jane's shoulder-length brown hair, normally worn clipped back by a tortoiseshell slide, into a sleek swingy flipped-up American long bob.

Anita had also made up Jane's eyes for her, shading the lids with a subtle blend of brown and bronze and pencilling a line of deep green along the inside of her lower lids to emphasise the dark green of her irises.

When Jane had protested that this was going too far, Anita had said firmly, 'If it's OK for Princess Di, it's OK for you. You're not that much older than she is. Cut a dash for a change. Make the best of yerself.'

As in fact Jane was younger than the Princess of Wales, the comment had made her wince a little inwardly.

At one time, Anita's chirpy familiarity would have caused Mrs Chichester to raise her eyebrows in disapproving hauteur. But not any more. It was many years since the house had been run by a team of respectful maids. Since then Olivia Chichester had, of necessity, adapted to some of the ways of the modern world.

'Anita is quite right... cut a dash, my dear,' she had agreed.

So now, fashionably made up and wearing a dress which today would cost thousands of pounds, Jane was scarcely recognisable as the neat and tidy secretary at whom no one gave a second glance.

'I feel like Cinderella going to the ball,' she said, pleased at her transformation but also slightly nervous of appearing in public in a guise so far removed from her everyday self.

'Let's hope you meet your Prince Charming. There are sure to be a number of personable young men there. I dare say most of those on Crowthorne's staff are not interested in women...' said Mrs Chichester. 'But among the guests there should be some eligible men... sons escorting their mothers and so on. If you aren't back by ten, I shall assume one of them has persuaded you to *diner à deux*.'

'I 'ope that don't mean what it sounds like,' said Anita, with a giggle. 'She could get 'erself into trouble.'

At this she got ticked off by Winnie. 'You've made Miss Jane blush with your rude talk.'

'*Diner à deux* is French. It means to have dinner with one other person, usually a man,' said Mrs Chichester.

'Is that right? I must try that out at the salon,' said Anita. 'Sounds classy, a bit of French. I know some Italian . . . *ciao* and *arrivederci*! Oh, look at the time. I'd better be going. I'm 'aving *diner à deux* in McDonald's with Brad in 'alf an hour. Oh, thanks . . .' as Jane paid her for the hair-do.

'We'll see Mis' Jane safe in a taxi, Mis' Chichester,' said Winnie. 'Lookin' like a million dollars, she might get mugged, waitin' in the street on her own.'

Luckily it was a dry night so Jane did not have to worry about spoiling the black velvet shoes made to go with the dress. They were half a size too large. Although she was tall she did not have large feet. But with two pairs of insoles inside them the shoes fitted well enough for standing about at a private view. Her back, bare to just below her shoulder blades, was protected from the cold by a silver fox jacket.

Jane had no evening wrap of her own and would have preferred to go in her everyday coat rather than borrowing the fur. But Mrs Chichester had insisted. She had no patience with modern views on the subject. They had come close to having a row until, knowing it was bad for the old lady to become angry or agitated, Jane had backed down and agreed to wear the jacket.

'Let's 'ope you don't run into none of them anti-fur activists,' said Anita, as the three women left the house together. 'I don't 'old with trapping animals, but I don't like them activists neither. There's never no call for violence if you ask me.'

Presently, enjoying the unaccustomed luxury of going somewhere by taxi, Jane crossed her legs and smoothed the skirt of her dress, enjoying the sensuous softness of the velvet's fine silk nap.

The only things she was wearing which were her own were a pair of sheer black Lycra stockings, bought specially for tonight, and a chain-store bra. In order not to spoil the clinging lines of the dress, Mrs Chichester had presented her with a pair of French knickers of peach silk-satin trimmed with pale grey lace, bought long ago and never worn.

As Jane had only one piece of good jewellery of her own, the old lady had also insisted on lending her cultured pearl ear-drops and a pair of art deco clips. The stones were paste, not diamonds, but they were paste of the finest 1930s quality. Only an expert would know they were not the real thing.

As the taxi merged with the stream of traffic swirling round Marble Arch to enter Park Lane, the light from a street lamp caught the stone on Jane's right hand. But it shone with the deep violet glow of a fine amethyst, not the cold fire of diamonds or rhinestones.

The ring, an heirloom, had been intended to adorn her left hand, but now she wore it on the other, although in fact this was the first time it had been out of its box for several years. One day she would give it to her godchild. Apple, she hoped, would have more occasions on which to wear it than Jane herself had ever had.

From the Bayswater Road to Brook Street, off Bond Street, where Crowthorne's premises occupied two large adjoining Georgian houses, was not far.

But the journey took long enough for Jane to start feeling nervous and to regret being persuaded into this masquerade. For that, without question, was what tonight's outing was. She knew Winnie had not been exaggerating in describing her appearance as looking like a million dollars. Tonight, in her borrowed finery, she could pass for a rich man's daughter, sister or girlfriend.

But the furs and the dress and the hairstyle could only give her a veneer, not the innate self-assurance such women had. Despite the illusory glamour she was still Jane Taunton, one of the world's also-rans, someone whose life had gone wrong and would probably never go right, at least not in the way she had dreamed of, nine years ago, when Nick had put the amethyst ring on her finger.

By the time the cab turned into Brook Street, she had a swarm of butterflies in her tummy.

A purple and gold awning had been erected over the entrance to Crowthorne's premises. Where it extended to the edge of the kerb, taxis were queuing to let down their passengers. Tonight a purple drugget led across the pavement and up the steps to the doorway.

Just inside the entrance, a young man in a dinner-jacket was collecting people's invitation cards and another man was directing them to the separate cloakrooms for men and women.

Jane's fear that Mrs Chichester's silver foxes might be stolen was banished when she found that special coat-racks were provided. A plastic-covered wire cable was threaded through a sleeve of each coat and locked into position. There was no possibility of an expensive fur being removed by anyone but the possessor of the key.

She put hers in the inside pocket of her borrowed evening-bag.

In the washroom adjoining the cloakroom, she checked that, during the nervous ten minutes in the taxi, she hadn't absent-mindedly chewed off all the lipstick carefully applied by Anita. But it was still there, a deeper more vibrant red than the unobtrusive pink she usually wore.

All around her, women who had come with friends were chattering.

'Sally damn nearly broke her neck hunting with the Beaufort last Friday. I think she's mad to ride when she's pregnant, but she says she hasn't lost a baby yet...'

'My dear, why not go to Daniel? He's the only hairdresser in London who understands colour. I know some people swear by...'

'That's the *third* time one of Caroline's au pairs has got herself pregnant, would you believe? But Hugo's too mean to stump up for a proper nanny...'

Snatches of the conversations going on around her reinforced Jane's feeling that she was an intruder in a milieu far removed from her own. She might *look* as if she belonged among these drawling upper-crust women, but really she had no business to be here. This was not her world any more than it was Anita's.

On leaving the cloakroom she followed a woman in blue silk up the splendid curve of the staircase to a large room on the first floor where the guests were being announced and received by someone she recognised, from once seeing him on Mrs Chichester's television, as Sir Timothy Crowthorne, the chairman of the company. Presumably the woman beside him was his wife.

'Miss Jane Taunton.'

She stepped forward to shake hands with the distinguished-looking head of the firm.

'Delighted to see you, Miss Taunton.'

Clearly he had no idea who she was. She wondered why a man with a strong handshake had married a woman with a limp one. She had a vague recollection of Mrs Chichester telling her that it had been an alliance of two great merchant dynasties, not a love match.

Next, Jane was handed a copy of an expensive catalogue of the pictures on show. She recognised the painting on the cover as a famous portrait. As she was gazing at it a waiter approached with a tray of champagne.

'Thank you.' She smiled at him as she took a tulip-shaped glass of the gently fizzing wine.

The rooms where the pictures were displayed were spacious and included a huge ballroom at the back of the grander of the two houses. Here the largest paintings, lent by the owners of various stately homes, had been hung. But it was a collection of portrait miniatures painted on small pieces of ivory and hung in a small side-room which attracted Jane more than the grand portraits.

She was bending to study the details of an oval miniature, framed with half-pearls, of a young girl in a high-waisted dress when a voice behind Jane said, 'A colleague tells me your dress is unquestionably by Madeleine Vionnet.'

It was only the name Vionnet which made her realise the remark had been addressed to her. Straightening and turning round, she found a very tall man in a dinner-jacket smiling at her.

'How clever of your colleague to recognise it,' she said, trying to sound as self-possessed as the wearer of a Vionnet should be.

'She's an expert on the fashions of that period. I expect, if I introduce her, she'll be able to tell you the year the dress was made and possibly the names of the ladies who chose it from that season's collection. For the moment let me introduce myself. Adam Fontenay. I work in the department dealing with eighteenth and nineteenth century water-colours.'

'I'm Jane Taunton. How do you do?' With the catalogue tucked under her arm, she transferred her glass to her left hand and offered her right one to him.

Like the chairman, Adam Fontenay had a firm grip, but the chairman's handclasp had not made her pulse-rate quicken in the same way that it did now as long brown fingers closed over hers. His tan suggested a recent holiday in the sun.

She remembered Mrs Chichester saying, 'Let's hope you meet your Prince Charming.'

Here he was, the personification of the man she had dreamed of meeting but never really believed would materialise. Tall. Broad-shouldered. Dark-haired. About thirty-five. Not handsome, better than handsome. He had everything she liked in a man. Steady, intelligent eyes which happened to be grey. A large high-bridged nose. A smile which showed excellent teeth. The kind of chin usually indicative of a decisive, responsible character.

'Fontenay sounds French,' she said.

'Originally it was. My forebears were among the quarter of a million Huguenots who fled from France after the Edict of Nantes was revoked.'

Jane had dim memories of learning about the Edict at school, but she couldn't remember any details, except that the Huguenots had been Protestants in a Catholic country and, like all minorities, vulnerable to persecution.

But whatever his ancestors might have suffered, vulnerable this man was not. He carried himself with an assurance she wished she shared, completely at home in these surroundings, not like herself, an outsider pretending to be an insider.

'Is it Ms, Miss or Mrs Taunton?' he asked.

'Miss.' On impulse, she added, 'Rather than lumping married and single women together under the title Ms, I think it would have been more useful to introduce labels which distinguished married men from bachelors.'

'I'm unmarried,' he said. 'But even that information can be misleading when so many people live together . . . and sometimes have partners of their own as well as the opposite sex. If it interests you—and I hope it does—at present I have no close relationship, but those I've had have been with girls.'

The amused tone in which he said this made Jane flush slightly. Her remark had been prompted by her personal dislike of being addressed as Ms. It embarrassed her that he should think she wanted to know whether he belonged to someone. Although the glint in his eyes as he'd said, 'I hope it does,' suggested that he was ready to flirt with her.

'Now you know where you are with me. What about you?' he asked.

'I'm single too.'

'And unattached?'

'Yes.'

'I can't believe my luck.' He followed this rather dizzying remark by saying, 'Your glass is empty. Let me get you another.'

Placing his own glass on an antique side-table, he took hers from her hand and went in search of one of the several waiters who were circulating with trays of drinks.

Fearing his glass might damage the glossy patina of the console, and rather surprised that anyone working for Crowthorne's should put a glass down on the polished surface of a fine antique, Jane picked it up.

When he returned and saw her holding it, he said, 'You needn't worry. All the horizontal surfaces are protected by clingfilm, a trick used by a lot of people when they give parties and don't want their furniture spoiled by glass-rings.'

'Really? What a good idea!' She had to look very closely at the table to detect that it had been carefully covered with a transparent film of fine plastic.

As well as bringing her another glass of champagne, Adam Fontenay had brought a silver dish of savoury mouthfuls.

'Let's sit down and get to know each other,' he said, indicating a Chippendale camel-back sofa covered in yellow jacquard silk.

She could see no way to demur without sounding ungracious, and deep down she didn't want to. It was a long time since an attractive man had taken an interest in her. Years. She never met any men. The ones at work were all married and she never went out in the evening except to an evening class where most of the students were women.

At one time her sister had tried to find a husband for her, but none of the men she had produced had appealed to Jane. She wasn't interested in marriage for its own sake. She wanted to fall in love again. But the chance of that happening, now, at the age of twenty-seven, was a remote one.

Or so it had seemed until she found herself sitting on a sofa with a man who appeared to be as strongly attracted to her as she was to him.

'Now you know a good deal about me. Tell me about you?' he said. 'No, wait a minute... let me guess. You work on one of the glossies... *Vogue* or *Harpers & Queen*. You write about current fashion but you collect and wear vintage clothes like this lovely thing you have on tonight. You may also collect portrait miniatures. You share a flat in Chelsea with another girl and spend your weekends in Gloucestershire with your family. Your mother gardens and does needlework. Your father goes in for field sports and possibly farms.'

'I'm afraid you're wrong on all counts. Actually——'

She was about to correct his suppositions when suddenly—perhaps it had something to do with drinking champagne on an empty stomach—she thought, Why?

The truth was so dull and boring. Why not, just for this one night, be someone else... the sort of woman this gorgeous man might fall for?

'Actually my parents are dead and I... I live in Florence,' she said recklessly.

It was the first outright, outrageous lie she had ever told in her life and it was no sooner uttered than she regretted it.

Yet it had the desired effect. She could see he was far more interested than if she had told him the truth.

Jane had been strictly brought up by a father of Victorian rectitude. Now the stern code learned as a child was in conflict with long-repressed longings.

Part of her wanted to retract the uncharacteristic falsehood. But part of her wanted to hold his interest. And how could she do that if she admitted to being just one of London's many thousands of wage-slaves, working for a firm he would never have heard of, and not doing any of the things—riding, skiing, wind-surfing, travelling to exotic places—that he and his friends took for granted?

The odds were that she would never meet him again after tonight. Was it very wrong to pretend, just for a short time, that she lived in the Italian city which would be her first destination if ever she were able to travel?

'I envy you living in Florence... marvellous city,' he said, while she was wrestling with her Puritan conscience. 'What brings you to London?'

So then, having taken the first step off what her father had called the straight path of truth, Jane found herself sliding down the slippery slope Mr Taunton had warned her about.

'I... I'm spending a few days with my grandmother. She lives here. She has a dinner party tonight so she asked me to come in her place. As I only brought casual clothes with me, I borrowed the dress from her. She bought it in Paris in 1933.'

'What do you do in Florence?'

'I... I'm learning Italian.'

This was partly true. For some time she had been studying Italian at evening classes in the hope that one day she would be able to go to Italy, a country which had always fascinated her.

Before he could press her for more information about herself, they were approached by another older couple to whom he introduced her. While the husband was talking to Adam Fontenay, the wife explained to Jane that they had a collection of paintings which Adam had helped them to select. It was soon apparent that, although she was quietly dressed, they must be extremely rich and important clients.

Jane was wondering how she could discreetly efface herself when, to her surprise, Adam took her by the elbow and said to them, 'Would you excuse us? There's a painting I want to show Jane.'

As he steered her away, he said, 'You don't mind my calling you Jane, I hope?'

'Not at all. But I feel you should be concentrating on Mr and Mrs Waterford, not wasting time on someone who's neither a buyer nor a potential seller.'

He looked down at her, his fingers still lightly holding her elbow. 'You come into a third and equally important category... the beautiful recipients of beautiful things. So for you it's important to learn what you want to be given. Diamonds aren't necessarily a girl's best friend. A work of art is a better bet. But perhaps you already know that. Perhaps that was why you were gazing so intently at the portrait miniatures.'

Jane shook her head. 'It was just casual interest.'

'When are you going back to Florence?'

'Tomorrow.'

'In that case will you have dinner with me tonight... when this thing breaks up?'

She hesitated. 'Thank you... I'd like to.'

'Good. If I'm going to have you to myself later, I'd better not monopolise you now. Come and meet some other people.'

From then on it was like being at a party with an attentive host who made sure she was never stranded with no one to talk to and never stuck with a bore.

Afterwards he took her to Annabel's, a nightclub in Berkeley Square. Jane had heard of the place but had never imagined being taken there.

The cosy bar, its wood-panelled walls painted the colour of cantaloup melons and crowded with pictures, its sofas piled with cushions, was unexpectedly like Mrs Chichester's cluttered drawing-room.

They did not stay in the bar but went straight to the dining-room where the green glass shades on the table lamps were reflected in the polished brass cladding the massive pillars of what must once have been a wine cellar, or underground kitchens and sculleries.

While Crowthorne's had expanded to fill two fine town houses, Annabel's was in the basement of a house mainly occupied, so Adam told her, by a separate gambling club.

From the way the staff at Annabel's greeted him, she gathered he made full use of his membership. As it didn't seem the type of club where he would entertain clients of Crowthorne's—although she could be wrong about that—she concluded he came here with women.

As she had already eaten quite a lot of the delicious titbits provided by Crowthorne's, on being given the menu Jane looked for something light. Most of the à la carte dishes seemed to be rather substantial—rib of beef, chicken Kiev and grilled Dover sole caught her eye—and she certainly hadn't room for the three-course set menu.

'If I'd known I was coming here, I would have resisted the food at the view,' she said.

Adam looked up from his own inspection of the menu. 'The fact that you didn't made me hope you might be one of those rare women who is *not* on a permanent diet.' As he spoke, his grey eyes appraised what he could see of her figure from the other side of the immaculately damask-clothed table.

'I'm not dieting.' It was on the tip of her tongue to explain that, in a sedentary job, she seldom used enough energy to need a large meal, when she realised that telling him that might lead to awkward questions.

'Good. Then what about starting with whitebait followed by the Châteaubriand?' he suggested.

Jane wasn't sure what the Châteaubriand was, but as it was listed among the meats she concluded it must be an expensive cut of steak. After it, in brackets, was written 'deux cvts' which she took to mean it had to be ordered by two people.

If that was what Adam fancied, perhaps she ought to agree; yet she knew she could never get through a large piece of meat on top of what she had eaten already.

'I'm afraid that would be too much for me. I'd rather have the scrambled eggs and smoked salmon.'

'As a starter or as your main course?'

'As my only course.'

To her relief, he didn't argue, but nor did he change his intention to have two courses himself.

Giving the order, he said, 'My guest would like some *crudités* to nibble while I'm having the whitebait, and then she'll have the scrambled eggs and smoked salmon while I have an *entrecôte*. We'll share a green salad.' To the wine waiter, he added, 'A bottle of the house Chablis, please.'

'Very good, Mr Fontenay.'

The simple menu cards and the wine list were whisked away and they were left on their own.

After glancing round the dining-room where, as yet, there were only a few people eating, Adam said, 'You've been here before, I expect?'

She shook her head. 'Never.'

A lift of his eyebrow indicated surprise.

To prevent him pursuing the matter, she decided to start asking him about himself.

'What part of London do you live in?'

'I have a *pied-à-terre* at the top of a house in Albemarle Street. Too small to swing a cat in. My father's an antiques dealer in Suffolk. My mother died two years ago and he's very lonely without her so I try to get home at weekends and keep him company.'

Jane had a distant relation in the antiques trade in Suffolk—he was related to her mother and known in the family as Cousin Hector. Her parents, having spent most of their married life abroad, had had little to do with him. She didn't mention him to Adam.

While he ate his whitebait and she dipped sticks of celery and carrot into a piquant dip, they discussed the exhibition.

'I've been trying to think who you remind me of and now I've got it,' Adam said suddenly. 'You're very like a portrait I saw in a show at Colnaghi's a few years ago. I forget the name of the sitter but the artist was Sir Frank Bernard Dicksee, one of the great Victorian painters. The picture was in the catalogue. I'll hunt it up and have it photocopied for you. Who knows? It may have been a painting of one of your forebears.'

'I shouldn't think so,' said Jane. She felt certain that none of her forebears had ever been painted, certainly not by an important artist.

'It was lent by a private owner,' Adam went on. 'I remember the face clearly now, and you're extraordinarily like her. She was lovely,' he went on, looking intently at her.

Jane acknowledged the implied compliment with a slight smile which belied the considerable disturbance going on inside her.

'But what struck me about her,' he went on, 'was the contrast between the gentle expression in her eyes and her very determined, even obstinate chin. The details are coming back now. She was the daughter of a Member of Parliament and the wife of another MP. But although she was married, she had a curiously innocent look.'

Jane felt her colour rising under his scrutiny. 'There are definitely no MPs in my family background. I suppose you go to all the big art shows.'

'Most of them—yes. But I don't see much to compare with the superb art in Florence.' To her relief, he went on, 'If you haven't been here before, you may not know that the owner is the son of the artist Sir Oswald Birley.'

Relieved to have moved away from Florence, Jane said, 'I think I've seen one of his works... two men and two women, one with a ribbon round her throat and opera glasses in her hand.'

'*The Theatre Box*—that's the one. Sir Oswald's granddaughter, India Jane Birley, is also a gifted artist. It's interesting, isn't it, the way creative genes are transmitted, often jumping a generation or two?'

At this point their main courses arrived and Adam asked if she knew that the combination of scrambled eggs with smoked salmon was said to cure hangovers.

'Although I shouldn't think that's an affliction you know much about,' he added drily.

'No, it isn't,' she agreed. 'Have you had many?'

He didn't look like a drinker. No tell-tale threads of red marred the whites round his steel-grey irises. His jawline was taut, not jowly. He might live well, but there were none of the signs of excessive self-indulgence.

If she hadn't known his occupation, she would never have guessed it. He had the spare, muscular build of the men she had watched on television inching their way up some vertiginous rock face to an inaccessible mountain peak.

'Not since my early twenties,' said Adam.

After the main course and before the coffee came, they danced on the small crowded floor, dimly lit from below, to recorded music.

By now more people had come in and there were too many dancing to allow energetic movement. Adam held her close, but not in such a way that she felt uneasy about how he thought their evening together might end.

Although it was a long time ago, she had had enough experience of heavy breathing and wandering hands to know that nothing in Adam's behaviour indicated an intention to try luring her up to his eyrie in Albemarle Street.

And he must know that, staying with her grandmother as she had claimed to be, she was unlikely to invite him in when he took her home.

Until that moment she had been relaxing and enjoying herself, but the realisation that he would certainly expect to see her home jerked her back to reality.

If she let him escort her to her door he would know where she lived. He might find out who she really was and that what she had told him about herself was a fantasy of half-truths and total inventions.

Somehow she must give him the slip so that he would never discover he'd spent the evening with someone whose knowledge of Florence was culled from books, and whose life was conspicuously lacking in the glamour a woman would need to hold Adam Fontenay's interest for more than a few hours.

CHAPTER TWO

IT WAS about half-past eleven and they were having coffee when Adam was called to the telephone.

It seemed a heaven-sent chance for Jane to make her escape. But suppose he caught her as she was trying to slip out? What explanation could she give for such strange behaviour? It might be better to say she preferred to go home alone. He couldn't insist on accompanying her...or could he? He struck her as a man more accustomed to giving instructions than taking them, a man who liked his own way.

While she was vacillating, Adam came back and the chance was lost.

But then, to her infinite relief, he said, 'I'm afraid I'm going to have to bring this very pleasant evening to an abrupt end. Do you mind if I put you into a taxi and send you home by yourself?'

'Not at all. What's happened?' she asked.

'My father has been grappling with a burglar. He's not seriously hurt but he's seventy-three and it must have been a great shock. I think I should drive down tonight, not leave him on his own until tomorrow.'

'Yes, of course, you must go at once. I'll get my coat. In case there's a crowd in the cloakroom, why don't you get away now? The doorman will get me a taxi.'

'No, no, it's not as urgent as that. I need your telephone number. Here's my card. What's your number in Florence?'

It so happened that Jane knew the international code for Italy was 39 and, having checked the Milan code number for her boss a few days before, she was fairly certain the code for Florence was 55.

Feeling wretchedly deceitful, she said, '010...39...55...5566,' and watched him jot it in the back of his diary.

A few minutes later, intending to walk the short distance to his flat, he saw her into a taxi.

'Where to, sir?' asked the club's doorman, thinking Adam was going with her.

Jane gave an address in a street not far from where she lived.

'I'll call you when I'm back in London,' said Adam, as she settled herself in the nearside corner. He leaned into the taxi and held out his hand. When she gave him hers, instead of shaking it he kissed it, his lips brushing her knuckles. 'I've enjoyed this evening very much. I hope you have too. Goodnight, Jane...or perhaps I should say *arrivederci*.'

To her relief, the light was not on in Mrs Chichester's sitting-room when, after being redirected, the taxi driver dropped her at her real address.

That meant the old lady was reading in bed or watching a late show on TV, for she was an insomniac who rarely slept before one or two in the morning and only fitfully then.

Thankful to avoid immediate questioning about the evening, Jane tiptoed up the staircase.

By now Adam would be on his way to Suffolk. Unless his father lived in the extreme south of the county, it must be a drive of at least two hours, probably more, even at this time of night when traffic would be light.

Probably, after drinking champagne at the private view and rather more than half the bottle of wine which had accompanied their dinner, he ought not to be driving at all. Although when they parted he had seemed perfectly sober and capable of the swift reactions needed in an emergency.

Perhaps he would stop for more coffee *en route*, if the road to Suffolk had all-night diners. If he began to feel tired, he might pull off the road and have a nap, or wake himself up by stretching his legs in the fresh air.

Judging from his conversation, Adam's outlook on life was a mixture of tolerance, humour and what her boss called horse-sense. It was something she would never find out, but she felt sure that Adam's car would not be a flamboyant sports model and although he might sometimes drive fast it would never be at a speed which exceeded the safe or legal limit.

Usually a sound sleeper, that night Jane slept as fitfully as Mrs Chichester. This might have been partly because she was not accustomed to eating a meal late at night, but the main reason was that she had an uncomfortable conscience.

Her behaviour during the evening had been completely out of character. Wiles, lies, pretence weren't part of her nature. Until tonight the only deception she had practised had been to help someone else, at a great cost to herself.

Going over the evening in her mind, she was forced to conclude that she must have been slightly tight. What else could have made her behave in such a mad reckless way?

There was no telephone in her flat but next morning, at the office, several times she was on the point of looking up Adam's father's number in Suffolk and, if Adam answered, first enquiring how his father was and then explaining and apologising.

But each time her courage failed her. And really what was the point? Even if he were prepared to overlook her behaviour, there could be no future in it. Once he found out the unexciting, un-special person she really was, he wouldn't want to pursue the friendship. And if, by some miracle, he did, sooner or later she would have to tell him about Nick. And that would be the end of that.

'Thank you for leaving the catalogue in a bag on my doorknob. Winnie brought it to me when she came. All day I've enjoyed looking at those lovely faces immortalised by the great portraitists,' said Mrs Chichester, when Jane entered her sitting-room that evening. 'Now tell me about the private view. Did you enjoy it?'

'Very much.'

Jane described Sir Timothy's wife's unbecoming dress, the famous people she had recognised, the mushroom caps stuffed with walnuts and cheese, the fresh figs wrapped in prosciutto, the wonderful flowers, the diamond brooches and other jewels, the delicious gusts of expensive scents, and every other detail of the evening she could remember.

'And afterwards? You came straight home? No, you would have come in to see me. You met someone . . . you went on somewhere.'

'Yes, I had dinner at Annabel's.'

'Annabel's! That's a very smart place... very expensive. Who is your beau?'

Jane mustered a laugh. 'He's not a beau, Mrs Chichester... just a passing acquaintance. I doubt if I'll hear from him again.'

I know I won't, she thought disconsolately.

And because she could not trust her kind old friend not to matchmake if she were told Adam's name and his connection with Crowthorne's, she was forced to give him a false name, John Keynston, and to pretend that he had been someone from out of town who now would be back where he came from.

Rather to her surprise, the old lady did not query the wisdom of dining alone with a stranger. Perhaps she thought that his presence at a Crowthorne's function was an adequate guarantee that he was an acceptable person, or that not much harm could befall a girl during dinner at Annabel's.

'Did he bring you home?' she enquired.

'No, he... he had a train to catch and had left himself short of time.'

Regretting the need for yet another fabrication, Jane changed the subject by asking which of the portraits Mrs Chichester liked best.

Later, before she went upstairs, the old lady said, 'At any rate you had a nice evening out which will have done you good. A girl of your age needs more fun than you have, my dear. I believe you allow an act of youthful indiscretion to weigh too heavily on you. Don't be too stern with yourself. We all make mistakes, you know, and yours was more forgivable than most.'

On impulse, Jane went to her and said, 'You don't know how much your friendship has meant to me. To be able to talk to you... confide in you... has meant more than I can say.'

'My dear child, it's I who should be grateful. Not many of your contemporaries would be as kind and patient with a decrepit old duck like me. Don't think I don't appreciate all you do for me. I only wish I could leave this house to you, Jane. But my husband wanted it to go to his nephew after me. Little did my darling Edgar guess what an unhelpful, selfish man Maurice would turn out to be. He and his wife never come near me, as you know. But they'll descend like vultures as soon as I'm dead. They know the terms of Edgar's will. As soon as my funeral's over they'll give all you poor girls notice and have the place put up for sale.'

'In that case you must make a determined effort to reach your centenary,' Jane said, smiling.

'Yes, if only I could outlive Maurice, I *could* leave the house to you,' said the old lady, chuckling at the prospect. 'He doesn't need it. You and the others do. Although I would much rather see you happily married than taking over from me. Off you go, my dear. You look tired from last night's late night. We'll talk again tomorrow.'

The days drew out. Spring came. Sometimes, thinking of Adam, Jane wondered what if any conclusion he had come to when he rang the number she had given him and discovered there was no such number or spoke to a puzzled Italian who had never heard of Signorina Taunton.

It might be that he thought she had muddled the number, or that he had misheard it.

Then, if he really had liked her as much as he'd seemed to, he would have done some detective work. But even the combined powers of Sherlock Holmes, Hercule

Poirot and Inspector Wexford would have failed to track down a guest who had attended the private view on someone else's ticket.

The only way they might meet again was by accident; and in a city the size of London the chance of two people who moved in different circles running into each other was small, not to say infinitesimal.

His was the world of men's clubs, of taxis and expensive shops, three-star restaurants, first nights, Hatchards bookshop, haircuts at Trumper's, weekends at country houses.

Hers was the world of the non-executive office worker; of queuing for buses or being squashed in the Underground in the rush-hour, of luncheon vouchers and sandwich bars, chain-stores, sunbathing in the park on fine weekends.

She spent Easter with Alice and Bill and the children. Her god-daughter had decorated an egg for her. It was a hen's egg. Her father had blown out the yolk so that Apple could paint it with blue flowers with yellow centres.

'Darling, it's lovely. I shall keep it with my special treasures,' she said, hugging her.

It seemed to her that the child was rather subdued, perhaps weary of the boisterous horse-play and constant teasing from the more extrovert members of the family.

Not long after her Easter break, Jane was surprised to receive a letter from old Cousin Hector, who had obtained her address by ringing her sister. He wrote:

> I should like you to come and see me. The sooner the better. I cannot accommodate you here but the

pub in the village does B and B very reasonably. Business is bad and I no longer have a telephone. Arrange your accommodation with the landlord of the Trowel and Hammer. He will let me know when to expect you. I have my lunch there most days.

The following weekend Jane travelled to Suffolk by train and thence to the village of Long Goosebeck by a bus which dropped her outside the pub where she was putting up.

The landlord was busy and it was his wife who took her upstairs to a small clean room on the first floor, and showed her where the bathroom was.

'He's a character, is Mr Beccles... eccentric, some people call him. Very hot-tempered on occasion, but as gentle as a lamb most of the time,' she told Jane. 'It's my belief he's not too well at the moment. Doesn't eat hearty like he used to. Doesn't drink much neither these days. Not that he ever was one to take more than he should. Always knew when to stop. Not like some of the young 'uns. Drink to get drunk, some of 'em. And then they start looking for trouble. It's not easy running a public house these days, I can tell you.'

Having arrived too late to join Cousin Hector for lunch in the bar, Jane unpacked her belongings before setting out to follow the landlady's directions for finding his shop.

The village had grown up round a large expanse of common land crossed by the stream called the goose beck. The pub, post office and police house were at one end. Most of the shops including Antiques and Curios were at the other.

A sign on the glazed door said 'CLOSED' but Jane rang the bell and presently saw Cousin Hector shuffling out of a room at the back. As he unlocked the door, she was surprised to see that he was much shorter than she was. His face reminded her of a guinea-pig.

He seemed equally surprised by her size. 'My word, what a beanpole you are. Come in. I'm just making tea. Will you take a cup?'

The interior of the shop was a higgledy-piggledy, dusty jumble of stuff which looked as if it had been there forever.

The back room was much the same except that it had a shabby but comfortable armchair and an upright chair at a table.

'Sit down. I shan't be long.' He disappeared into a scullery, soon to return with tea things, including the remains of a cake, on a tea-stained tin tray.

He was pouring tea from an earthenware pot with a knitted cosy over it when someone else rang the bell.

'See who it is, m'dear, will you? If it's someone in the trade, I'm in. If it's anyone else, tell them I'm having forty winks and you can't disturb me.'

Jane was halfway across the shop when her heart gave a violent lurch. The man who was waiting outside had had his back to the door. When he turned and peered through the long-unwashed panes, she recognised him immediately.

It was Adam Fontenay.

'Who is it?' asked Cousin Hector, when she shot back inside the inner room.

'He looks like a dealer. Where is your loo, Cousin Hector?'

'One day I had a bit of luck,' he went on. 'Do you know who Fabergé was?'

'Was he a Russian jeweller?' she ventured uncertainly.

The old man nodded. 'That's right. . . jeweller to Tsar Alexander III and supplier of knick-knacks to our own Queen Alexandra and most of the other crowned heads of the day. Well, I once bought a pretty little ornament made by the great man himself. . .a cat carved from blue-grey chalcedony with diamond eyes and platinum whiskers. It was the sort of piece which, in the ordinary way, I'd have put in the bank as insurance against hard times. But there'd been some trouble with the drains and expensive repairs to the shooting brake I ran then. I was a bit short of cash. So I put the cat in the window priced at two hundred and fifty pounds. The damn fool of a woman thought it was marked two pounds fifty and she sold it for that to young Fontenay.'

'But surely, if he showed it to his father, old Mr Fontenay must have known it was a mistake?'

'The young 'un knew that himself. Do you think the son of the biggest dealer for miles around needs to be told that you can't buy a piece of Fabergé for fifty bob? Course he knew. Sharp as a basket of monkeys. . .always was. He works up in London for Crowthorne's, sowing his wild oats with all those pretty society girls they have working on the front counter. One of these days his old man will kick the bucket and he'll have to settle down and take over the business. Meanwhile he's having a ball, as they say nowadays. But for all their grand airs and graces the chap is a thief and his father condoned the theft. There's no getting away from that.'

'Did you go to see his father when you found out what had happened?' Jane asked.

'Refused to see me...had me thrown off the premises. Guilty conscience, you see. Knew damn well his boy had fleeced me. That's why I enjoyed throwing him out of my place just now. Tit for tat. Not that he'll care. I wonder why he wanted that clock. It's not worth a light. Unless he knows something I don't, which isn't very likely. I've been in the trade as long as his father...longer. There's not much I don't know.'

For the rest of the afternoon she listened to his reminiscences of how he had started dealing in the 1930s when the problem was not finding stock, but finding customers to buy it.

'Not many people were interested in antiques in those days. Now every other person you meet has a collection of something or other. But in those days collectors were few and far between. Eighteenth-century furniture was the thing then. Anything Victorian was rubbish. Even Regency pieces wouldn't sell except to a discerning few.'

Jane listened and made fresh tea and sat down to listen again. But part of her mind was thinking about Adam.

It was unlikely he had recognised her from one brief glimpse through the murky glass panes of the door. Even if he had seen her more clearly, in her sweater and jeans with her hair pulled back from her face and very little make-up she bore only a slight resemblance to the girl he had taken to Annabel's.

It was on the tip of her tongue to ask Hector how far Great Maybrugh was from Long Goosebeck. Then she decided it would be tactless to remind him of his two *bêtes noires*. She would ask the people at the pub.

It was dusk when she left the shop to return to the Trowel and Hammer. Hector had agreed to her suggestion that they should have an evening meal there.

It was only as she was crossing the bridge across the stream that she realised the old man hadn't yet explained why he had summoned her to come and see him.

'There was a gentleman asking for you earlier, Miss Taunton,' said the publican's wife when, the next day, Jane returned from morning service at the village church.

Hector had told her that he didn't get up until noon on Sundays and, on impulse, she had gone to church for the first time in years. It had been curiously soothing to breathe in the forgotten aroma of beeswaxed pews, dusty hassocks, camphor-scented Sunday best clothes, handkerchiefs sprinkled with lavender water.

'A gentleman? Who?' she asked.

'Young Mr Fontenay from the Manor at Great Maybrugh. He didn't ask for you by name. He came in for a Heineken and chatted about this 'n that. Then he said he'd seen a young lady in Mr Taunton's shop and was you a new assistant? I said no, you was a relative come to visit the old chap. Then he asked if you was staying here—well, you wouldn't hardly stay there, the state the shop's in—and said he would call back later. I couldn't quite make it out. I mean if he don't know you, what could he be wanting, I wonder?'

'I've no idea,' said Jane. 'Did you tell him my name?'

'Yes, I did. There seemed no harm in it. Did I do wrong?'

'No, not at all, Mrs Westward. Does the village have a taxi? I thought a breath of sea air might do Mr Beccles good... that we'd go to the coast for lunch today.'

'We don't have a taxi, I'm afraid. Can you drive a car yourself?'

Jane said that she could. Nick had taught her to drive and she still had a licence because sometimes, when staying with Alice, she ran errands by car for her sister or took the children out for the day to give her sister a rest from her family's clamour.

'I'll have a word with my hubby. Perhaps you can borrow our car. You look like a careful driver.'

The landlord had no objection. It was Hector who wasn't keen on having his routine disrupted by a jaunt to the coast. But, foreseeing an embarrassing scene if Adam came back while she and the old man were having lunch at the Trowel and Hammer, she jollied him gently but firmly into agreeing.

On the Westwards' advice they went to a small hotel which was open to non-residents and there had a Sunday lunch which reminded Jane of the meals served at her school. Her father and mother had both been missionary teachers. From the age of ten to sixteen, she and Alice had been boarders at a school for girls whose parents were overseas.

'You haven't explained why you wanted to see me, Hector?' she said, cutting a thick slice of overcooked beef coated with glutinous gravy.

'I'm for the high jump,' he answered. 'Going to kick the bucket, my doctor tells me. No need to look upset. We all have to go some time. I've had a good run... seventy-seven next birthday.'

His manner matter-of-fact, he told her what was the matter with him and that, at his age, no treatment was likely to prolong his life for more than a few months.

'At least it's likely to be quick. Shouldn't like a lingering end. Short and sharp, that's the best way to go.

Which brings me to the reason I sent for you. How would you like to take over the business . . . such as it is?'

'But Hector, I don't know anything about antiques.'

'Neither did I when I started. You're young and you seem intelligent. Pick it up as you go along. You'll have a roof over your head. The house isn't mortgaged. I bought it for six hundred pounds thirty years ago and I've never raised money on it. Anyway, it's yours when I go. I've no one else to leave it to.'

After lunch they walked along the seafront, the old man holding her arm. He smelt like the lonely old men who frequented the reading-rooms of public libraries. She wondered how long it was since he had last had a bath or taken his suit to be cleaned. But she liked him and felt sorry for him.

'Why don't you sell the house and spend the time left to you in a comfortable nursing home?' she suggested. 'Or you could go on a cruise, if you feel up to it.'

'No, no, I'm set in my ways. I'd rather stay put till I snuff it. I've had enough of this world. I'm quite keen to see what the next one is like.'

Presently he said he would like to have a nap in the back of the Westwards' car. Jane sat on a bench not far from where she had parked it and thought about his proposal.

He still made a little money out of the business, but without his old-age pension it wouldn't be enough to live on. The sensible thing to do, if he insisted on leaving the house and shop to her, would be to sell it. If Hector couldn't make a living, what chance had she?

She had been trying not to think about Adam because when she did her insides churned with apprehension.

Evidently he had recognised her and meant to demand an explanation of her behaviour in London.

Could it be true that he and his father had, in effect, defrauded Hector of a large sum of money? It seemed a very shabby way for a rich dealer and his son to behave towards someone many rungs below them in the hierarchy of the antiques trade.

When they returned to Long Goosebeck, she dropped Hector outside the shop and drove the car into what had once been a stable-yard at the back of the pub.

'Did Mr Fontenay come in at lunchtime, Mrs Westward?' she asked, after thanking the publican for the loan of the car.

'No, he didn't. Perhaps he'll come in this evening.'

There were always freshly made sandwiches under a Perspex dome on the bar. Jane took some across to the shop for a picnic supper with Hector. She stayed there, talking to him until after closing time. The Westwards had given her a key to let herself in by the back door.

There was no one about as she crossed the green. The livid glow of television screens showed through unlined curtains at some windows. The chip shop, which, the night before, had been crowded with young people, was closed. Lines of parked cars spoiled the look of the green but showed that its inhabitants were more prosperous than when Hector had settled there, at which time only he, the doctor, the vicar and one or two landowners had been able to afford cars.

As she approached the pub, wondering if she could borrow the car again tomorrow, the door of one of the parked cars suddenly opened a couple of yards ahead of her.

Jane stopped short on an indrawn breath. For a second or two it was the instinctive fear of every city-dwelling woman out by herself after dark which held her rooted where she stood. Then as she recognised the tall figure of Adam Fontenay that fear was replaced by a different kind of trepidation.

'I've been waiting for you, Miss Taunton,' he told her. 'As I seem to be *persona non grata* with your choleric relation, I thought it advisable to wait until I could talk to you alone. You owe me an explanation.'

CHAPTER THREE

'IT'S late and I'm tired,' Jane protested.

'So am I...tired of trying to fathom why you couldn't tell me straight out that you didn't want to see me again. I've been given the brush-off before but never by your devious method. I want to know why you put me to the trouble and expense of calling a number in Florence which wasn't your number. Was it your idea of a joke?'

What could she say? How could she possibly explain?

As she stood there, dumb with embarrassment, Adam put both hands on her shoulders and gave her an impatient shake.

'Answer me!'

Jane stiffened, her chin coming up and her eyes beginning to flash.

'Perhaps I had a premonition that under the suave veneer there was a bad-tempered boor. Please take your hands off me!'

As he had his back to the moon which was still fairly low in the sky, it was difficult to see the expression in his eyes. But his hands didn't leave her shoulders. If anything his fingers tightened.

Long ago Nick had shown her how to defend herself if she were attacked. She'd forgotten most of the tricks he'd taught her. It was largely instinct which made her swing up both arms to strike out sideways with her forearms.

The manoeuvre was partly successful in that it did succeed in dislodging Adam's hands from her shoulders. But the next instant he had both her wrists locked in his powerful fingers and had pinioned her arms behind her. Jerked close to his tall body, she found herself pressed against him as closely as if they were embracing, and there wasn't a thing she could do about it.

Then, as abruptly as he had grabbed her, he let her go and stepped back.

'I beg your pardon. I shouldn't have done that. I lost my temper.' There was a pause before he added, 'I won't bother you again. Goodnight.'

Before she had recovered from the shock of being imprisoned in his arms, he had climbed back into his car, slamming the door with a force which might not have seemed loud by day but sounded very loud at night.

She was still standing where he had left her when he drove away.

When Jane told Mrs Chichester the reason why Cousin Hector had summoned her to Suffolk, the old lady said, 'Poor man: a lonely life by the sound of it. Did he never have a wife, or children, or even a partner of his own sex?'

'I don't think he's ever had any close relationships, but he doesn't strike me as lonely.'

'Why don't you give up your job and go and make him comfortable for his last months? It would be a challenge to put the shop to rights and try your luck as a dealer. You need a stimulus, Jane. You're drifting along in a dull job. Life is too precious to be wasted. Why not take this chance that's been offered?'

'I'll think about it,' said Jane.

Her memory disconcertingly sharp, Mrs Chichester said, 'You might run into that nice man who took you to Annabel's. He lived in Suffolk, didn't he?'

Jane turned away to hide her blush. 'I don't think that's very likely.'

The mention of Adam revived the disturbing feelings she had experienced in his arms. She had almost forgotten what it felt like to be held close by someone taller and stronger. Not that Nick had been as tall or as powerfully built as Adam. He had been thin and wiry; a young man hiding his uncertainty under a brash, cocky manner, a tough guy with a soft heart.

'Well, whatever you decide, at least now you've somewhere to go if anything happens to me,' said Olivia Chichester.

Two weeks later she died in her sleep.

She had been right about her nephew. When the funeral was over, and the will had been read, he gave all the tenants notice.

Jane moved to Suffolk in the middle of June and lived at the Trowel and Hammer while she made Hector Beccles' back bedroom fit to be slept in.

The whole house needed a thorough sorting-out and spring-clean and she set to work with an enthusiasm she hadn't felt for a long time.

In addition to the John Smart portrait miniature and a wardrobe of vintage clothes, Olivia Chichester had bequeathed various pieces of furniture to her, much to the annoyance of Maurice and his tight-lipped, disapproving wife.

For the first week, Jane couldn't get used to the fact that she had left London forever.

London, the mecca of her teens, the city of exciting opportunities. London, the prison of her twenties, the city she was thankful to escape. Even if she couldn't make a go of the antiques shop, she would never go back. There were secretarial jobs in the provinces which might not pay quite as much as those in the capital, but, as living expenses were lower, it made little difference.

Not long after her arrival, an auction was held at a large country house in the area.

'There'll be dealers from all over England competing for the best stuff. Even the junk will sell for ten times what's its worth,' said Hector. 'But it'll be a good test of whether you've got an eye for quality or not. We'll both go to the view, but separately. Make careful notes of everything you fancy and what your top bid would be. Then I'll tell you what I would have bought.'

Jane set out for the auction on a bicycle borrowed from the Westwards, whose son, a partner in a garage, was looking out for a second-hand car for her. Hector had sold his old runabout when his doctor had said he must stop driving.

Bicycling along country lanes on a fine summer morning made her feel glad to be alive and beginning a new phase of her life. Unless Hector's health deteriorated—and her coming seemed to have made him look and feel better—she was hoping it would be possible to have Apple to stay for several weeks in the school holidays.

The auction was to be held on two successive days the following week. The house was a run-down great barn of a place, the property of an aged admiral who had died without heirs. His executors had put the property into the hands of a local firm, Osborne and Deal.

Jane was a little surprised that, as the Fontenay family had probably been on social terms with the admiral, the contents were not being auctioned by Crowthorne's. One of the things she had learned from Hector was that antiques dealers were always particularly keen to buy goods which had never been on the market before. When furniture had been in private hands since it was new, it fetched premium prices.

Catalogues were on sale at the door. She bought one and began to work her way through it. She had come early and not many people were there yet. In each room an auctioneers' porter in a blue overall was keeping an eye on things, sometimes unlocking the glass cases in which small pocketable items had been placed for safekeeping.

Jane was admiring a pair of brilliant blue and gold Coalport cornucopiae, thinking how pretty they would look brimming with white freesias, when a voice which made her heart lurch said, 'Good morning. You're living here now, I hear.'

Adam was not alone. Standing beside him was an elderly man who was obviously his father. Once as tall as his son but now rather stooped, the older man had the same air of distinction and authority.

'Good morning.' She did not smile.

Adam said, 'May I introduce my father, Colonel Fontenay? Dad, this is Miss Taunton...Jane. We met at the private view of "Two Hundred Years of Beautiful Women".'

'Ah, yes, I remember,' said the colonel, shaking hands. But whether he meant he remembered the exhibition or something his son had told him about her was not clear.

'Jane is helping Hector Beccles to sort out his shop,' said Adam. 'I believe they are distant relations. Is that piece of gossip correct?' he asked her.

'Yes, it is. Does information always circulate so fast in this part of the world?'

'Rumours and counter-rumours buzz about like bees over wallflowers,' said the colonel, smiling at her. 'Are you here in a professional capacity or as a private buyer, Miss Taunton?'

'I'm not a dealer,' she told him. 'And my cousin tells me the prices will be sky-high.'

'Undoubtedly. There are some very fine pieces which have been in the family for centuries. Crowthorne's have lost a lot of commission.' He directed a quizzical glance at his son. 'Unfortunately Adam was caught trespassing on this estate about twenty years ago and Crowthorne's have suffered in consequence.'

Whatever her personal feelings were towards Adam—and she wasn't sure what she did feel—Jane was obliged to acknowledge that he took the quip very well.

'My father maligns me,' he said, with a good-humoured grin. 'It's true that, aged about fourteen, I was caught rabbiting on the admiral's land and threatened with everything from prosecution to keel-hauling. But the reason that Osborne and Deal are handling the sale is because they are also in charge of selling the house. The executors are local men who believe in supporting local firms. Do you like auctions, Jane?'

She thought better of admitting it was the first she had attended. If she did take over Hector's business, it wouldn't do for the word to go round on the grapevine that she was a green-horn who knew nothing.

Because of their social aplomb, it was easy to forget that these two men were implicated in what, by any standards, fell short of honourable conduct over the Fabergé cat.

'Yes, I do, even though I don't expect to buy much, if anything, at this one. Excuse me. I'd better get on.' With a polite smile for the colonel, she turned away.

It took her all morning to appraise every lot. To her dismay, when she was ready to go home, she found her back tyre was flat. Hoping the puncture was a slow one, she unclipped the bicycle pump.

Before she reached the end of the drive, the tyre had deflated again. Fortunately the saddle-bag contained a repair kit and she turned the bike upside-down and began to lever the tyre off.

She had scarcely begun when a car pulled up behind her and a man in a tweed sports coat and corduroy trousers got out.

'Having trouble? Perhaps I can help. That's a job you can break your nails on.'

'It's very kind of you, but my nails aren't long ones and I don't want to stop you getting home to your lunch.'

'I was only going to the pub for a sandwich. I'm Dick Osborne, the auctioneer. And you, I believe, are old Hector Beccles' great-niece.'

'A more distant relation than that. My name's Jane Taunton.' As they shook hands, she added, 'News certainly does travel fast in Suffolk.'

'Dealers are tremendous gossips. Are you in the trade?' He took the lever from her and began with quick expert movements to free the tyre from the wheel.

'I may be going to take over Hector's business. It all depends,' she said cautiously.

'On what?'

'On whether I think I can make a go of it. I've come to Suffolk from London. It's like moving to another country. I like it much better here, but maybe, as an outsider, I'll find it hard to make ends meet.'

'It would have been easier way back when I was a kid. The stuff I could buy with my pocket money would cost a good income today. Stock is thin on the ground and getting thinner. But it's never been an easy living...for the trade or for auctioneers. When there was plenty of stock there wasn't the money or the interest. Now it's gone to the other extreme. Hey, this is a nasty rip. You must have tangled with a nail or something on your way here.'

While he dealt with it for her, she studied him. About the same age as Adam...middle thirties. Reddish-brown curly hair, still thick but with a lot of grey in it. Light blue eyes. Freckles on a blunt nose and on the backs of his hands. He reminded her of her brother-in-law, not in looks but because both men exuded an air of capable kindness.

'Hmm...I'm not too happy about this. You really need a new tube. Look, let's shove it in the back of the car and I'll run you back to Goosebeck.'

Taking her assent for granted, he picked up the bike and carried it round to the rear of his large estate car, the back part of which was wired off, suggesting that dogs often travelled in it.

'How d'you get on with the old boy?' he asked, on the way along.

'Very well. Why do you ask?'

'He has the reputation of being a bit cantankerous. You're not living in the house with him, are you?'

'Not yet, but I shall be as soon as I've sorted it out a bit more. Where do you live, Mr Osborne?'

'Call me Dick. Everyone does. I used to have a house in Pondford until three years ago my wife died. It was difficult to get anyone suitable to look after the house and my boy. So now we live with my parents. They have plenty of room and they both adore Tommy. It's working out well.'

'How old is Tommy?'

'Ten. Goes to the local school and potters around with me in the holidays. He's down to go to my old school when he's thirteen. I shall miss him like hell. He's a scamp at times but a nice kid.' After a pause, he added, 'My wife and I had known each other since pram days. We were very happy. When so many people can't get along together, it's hard to accept philosophically that we could have made it to our golden wedding but didn't because she got ill.'

Jane said, 'I know how you feel. The boy I was going to marry was killed on a motorbike when he was only nineteen. It wasn't his fault. He swerved to avoid a woman pushing a pram into the road without looking. The alternative was hitting a lorry.'

He glanced at her. 'Bloody back luck. It's odd...I think I knew you would understand. I don't usually talk about Sally, even to people who knew her. Least of all to them. They get embarrassed. They don't understand that part of the pain is not being able to talk about someone who's died. Have you found that?'

'Yes, very much...at first. I'm over it now. It was quite a long time ago. Nine years. And we were never together like you and your wife. That must leave a much worse gap.'

'A great yawning void... a black hole I wished would swallow me up. If I could have gone away... but because of Tommy I couldn't. I just had to sit it out. But, like you, I'm over the worst now. And I've got him and he's very like her. Funny how boys seem to take after their mothers and girls after their fathers.'

He had taken a different route from the one she had come by and now they were passing through a village with a pub called the Lamb with a board outside it announcing 'SANDWICHES, HOT SNACKS'.

'How about having a bite here? If you're not in a hurry to get back?'

'All right, as long as it's Dutch treat.'

'Certainly not. I'll be making plenty of money out of your buyer's premium if you're going to stick around. As Mr Beccles has probably told you, we have auctions every other week where the prices don't hit the roof as they will for the admiral's stuff.'

When Hector, who had been given a lift to view the auction by a dealer who was a crony of his, compared Jane's theoretical bids with his own, his verdict was that she had a good eye for quality but not much idea of prices.

Having no intention of bidding, he did not go to the auction but sent her along 'to watch the big boys at work'.

Feeling sure that Colonel Fontenay would be one of the big dealers present, and wondering if Adam would also be there, Jane again set off on her bike.

This time, when she arrived, the long drive was lined with cars and a large marquee had been erected on the lawn. She was hovering in the entrance, looking for a place to sit, when Dick came up to her.

'Hello, Jane. I've kept a seat for you where you'll get a good view. This way.'

He took her arm, steering her round the aisle next to the canvas walls to the other side of the huge tent. She was conscious of local eyes looking with curiosity at this stranger who was receiving special attention from the auctioneer.

'How about having dinner with me on Friday night?' he murmured, close to her ear. 'Tonight and tomorrow I'll be resting my larynx. But on Friday I can relax and live it up on the proceeds. We're hoping this stuff is going to fetch record prices.'

'I'd like that. Thank you.'

'It's a date. I'll pick you up about seven.'

Settled in her vantage-point, Jane scanned the rows of heads for a white-haired head next to a dark one. She had expected to see them in the front row but they were several rows back. She wondered if Adam had noticed Dick escorting her to a reserved seat.

The auction began with a short speech by Dick's father, who had founded the business but no longer conducted sales. His opening remarks were received with applause and then Dick took his place and gave a brief explanation of the way the sale would be conducted. Then he called for the first lot and two porters lifted one of a set of French *bergère* chairs into view.

All morning bidding was brisk and the gavel came down on prices even higher than Hector's estimates.

At a quarter to one Dick announced a break for lunch. 'We'll resume sharp at two fifteen. Thank you, ladies and gentlemen.'

Jane had brought a packet of sandwiches, a flask of coffee and a book about antique furniture from Hector's private reference library. While other people drove to pubs or bought snacks from a mobile tea-stall which had been permitted to park at the front of the house, she set out across the lawn to find a secluded spot in which to bone up what to look for and what to avoid.

All the garden's seats and statuary, even some antique watering-pots and old-fashioned china plant labels, were included in lots to be sold on the second day. But there had been no rain for some days so she settled herself on the grass with her back against a tree trunk.

After wondering who would buy the house, she thought that if it were still up for sale when Apple came they might follow Adam's example and do a little harmless trespassing. The neglected grounds—the admiral had been over ninety with no staff but an ancient odd-job man—were the perfect place for an imaginative child to play fanciful games.

'Do you mind if I join you?'

Her eyes closed against the strong sunlight, Jane gave a violent start. Looking even taller than usual from her seat on the ground, Adam was holding his blazer slung over one shoulder. He had also taken off his tie and the collar of his shirt—finely checked blue and white cotton with the same crisp freshness that a gingham cloth gave to a café table—was unbuttoned. He had folded back the cuffs, showing several inches of sinewy forearm, the skin brown under a light veiling of dark hair.

She remembered the weight of his hands on her shoulders and his furious, 'Answer me!'

'This is a very large garden. There are lots of other pleasant spots,' she said pointedly.

He went down on his haunches, the lightweight pale grey gabardine of his trousers tightening over his long thighs.

'I apologise again for the other night. But I think, if you're honest, you'll agree there was provocation. No one likes to be made a fool of. If that wasn't your intention, why not explain what your intention was?'

She sighed. 'All right: I'll try. That night was a kind of... masquerade for me. I only went at the insistence of the friend who should have been there. She wasn't well enough to go and she wanted me to report back. She also lent me the dress and everything else I was wearing.'

Taut nerves were making her throat dry. She unscrewed the top of her flask which was capped with two plastic cups. 'Would you like a cup of coffee?'

'Thank you.' He lowered himself into a sitting position on the grass beside her, tossing his blazer casually aside.

Jane filled a cup and passed it to him. 'When you asked me about myself, I thought the truth was dull and that it would be more amusing to invent a persona to go with the Vionnet dress. I then discovered the truth of the saying: "O what a tangled web we weave, When first we practise to deceive". But it wasn't intended to be a confidence trick. I had no ulterior motive. It was just a silly impulse.'

'I see.' He sipped the coffee. 'The implication seems to be that, by the end of the evening, you were not greatly concerned about meeting again.'

'I—I didn't think, if you knew the truth about me, you would want to meet again.'

He lifted an eyebrow. 'Why not? Are you a call girl? A drug pusher? Offhand those are the only two things I can think of which would put me off you.'

'I'm not anything bad... merely not very interesting. Until I came here I was a secretary to the assistant manager of a trading company specialising in shipping, mineral production and the manufacture of bus and truck bodies.'

'And rather than tell me that you gave me a false telephone number? Come, come: I'm not buying that.'

'All right, don't. But it's the truth.'

Adam gave her a thoughtful look. 'If it is, you must have an incredibly low sense of your own value. Don't you ever look at yourself in a mirror? Even without the drop-dead number you were wearing that night, you're a very attractive girl. With plenty between the ears. I shouldn't have wanted to see you again if there hadn't been.'

She didn't know what to say to this except, 'Would you like a sandwich?'

'Thank you.' He took one from the packet she offered him. 'Mmm... this is good. What is it?'

'Ham, Brie and wholegrain mustard.'

He ate in silence for a while, saying finally, 'There's one way you can prove that it wasn't a brush-off.'

'How?'

'By having dinner with me again.'

'It's not as simple as that. Now there's Hector to consider. As you know, he doesn't like you.'

'To be frank, I'm not crazy about him. If you're going to let him dictate whom you do or don't see, you're going to have a sparse social life. I'm afraid the fact is the old boy makes a habit of roaring and ranting. He's made enemies of a lot of people you might enjoy knowing. I'm going back to London tonight but I'll be home again on Friday. How about Friday evening?'

'I'm engaged on Friday.'

'I see.' He didn't ask what she was doing on Saturday or Sunday. He just handed back the empty cup, rose to his feet with the ease of a man who kept his body in good condition, and said, 'Some other time, I hope.'

And with that he picked up his coat and walked away.

She watched him go, admiring his straight back and easy stride. She wished she had not accepted Dick's invitation. But even if she hadn't, it would have been very awkward, going out with someone Hector detested. She wished Adam hadn't glossed over the mutual dislike between himself and Hector. She ought to have asked him for his side of the story.

Although he was not as furious as he would have been if she had been dining with Adam, Hector was not pleased when he heard about her date with Dick.

'You don't want to get too thick with those Osbornes,' he said. 'I don't trust auctioneers. They're a fly bunch, up to more tricks than a basket of monkeys.'

'What sort of tricks?'

'Taking bids off the wall.'

'What does that mean?'

'It means if the bidding is slow, an unscrupulous auctioneer takes 'em from an imaginary bidder. Cleverly done, it's damned hard to detect.'

'Are Dick and his father suspected of doing it?'

'I didn't say that. I was speaking generally. But one thing I do advise you is not to leave bids with their clerk. If you can't get along to a sale, leave a bid with one of the porters. An auctioneer knows what bids the clerk has taken and if the bids from the floor only reach fifty pounds but you've left a bid of a hundred, that's what you'll pay. He's not going to let the lot go for fifty-two or fifty-five. Stands to reason, doesn't it? On your hundred he'll get more commission.'

'I suppose so.'

Having dinner with Dick on Friday at a country inn, Jane asked him if it were true that some auctioneers took bids off the wall.

'It was more likely to happen in the old days when, if there was no reserve, good things sometimes were knocked down for ludicrous prices. I don't think it happens much now. My father's never done it and nor have I. Dealers aren't always above reproach, you know,' he said drily.

'Are the Fontenays above reproach?'

'Good lord, yes. I should say so. Colonel Fontenay wouldn't do anything shady to save his life.'

'What about his son?'

'Adam's all right...very knowledgeable about paintings.'

'But you don't like him?' she ventured.

'I wouldn't say that. Where did you meet him?'

'At one of Crowthorne's exhibitions in London.'

'Did he make a pass at you?'

'No. Is that his reputation?'

'Used to be. As a matter of fact he helped my sister to get a job at Crowthorne's. She was mad keen to get to London. She fell for him, but he got bored and dropped her. She's OK now, happily married with two kids. But he gave her a bad time. I should be a bit wary of him, if I were you. He's had a lot of affairs and they've usually ended in tears. For the girls.'

CHAPTER FOUR

AT THIS point their conversation was interrupted by the arrival of his steak and her fish. By the time they had helped themselves to a shared dish of vegetables, either Dick had forgotten about Adam or chose to change the subject by asking about her life before she came to Suffolk.

It was a pleasant evening which ended soon after eleven when they said goodnight outside the Trowel and Hammer.

'Let's do it again soon,' he suggested, when she thanked him. 'That's if you'd like to repeat the exercise?'

His diffidence touched her. She said, 'Yes, very much,' wondering inwardly if it might be a mistake.

Why she felt this, she wasn't sure. Perhaps it was merely that, after years of not going out with men, two dates in successive weeks seemed going to the other extreme.

Later, in bed, she remembered his warning about Adam and wondered if she would heed it if Adam did ask her out again.

Whereas in London Jane had often woken in the night and lain awake wondering and worrying about the future, now at the end of the day she was usually too tired to read in bed and slept until roused by her alarm clock.

Perhaps it had something to do with the fresher, more bracing air of the east coast, or perhaps it was because she was using more physical energy than her job as a secretary had required.

Having sorted out a place to sleep, she began to tackle the ground floor. Hector had been warned against lifting anything heavy. So she asked a sturdy-looking schoolboy who lived near by if he would like to earn some extra pocket money helping her shift the larger pieces of furniture which Hector had allowed to accumulate even though they were too badly damaged or too junky ever to sell.

'Why did you buy them?' she asked him.

'Sometimes you have to buy things you don't want to get what you do want,' he told her. 'Anyway, you can never be sure what will sell. I've known people to pay a good price for something I wouldn't have as a gift.'

It was deeply satisfying gradually to make order out of chaos, Jane found. In drawers and inside cupboards which had previously been inaccessible, things came to light which Hector had forgotten he had put there.

In an old black lacquer workbox there was a cache of mother-of-pearl counters, many engraved with family crests. Some had been used for gambling, some for more innocent parlour games. In another box he had put aside the embroidered postcards sent by soldiers to their sweethearts during the First World War. In fading ink they carried messages such as, 'All my love until we meet again, dearest one'.

Jane disposed of the really junky furniture by asking Roy, her fourteen-year-old helper, to chop it up for firewood. Two or three pieces which were not a bad shape but marred by a shiny varnish finish she got him to strip in the back yard, having first asked his parents' approval for this operation.

Hector still had his main meal at the Trowel and Hammer and so did she. Although the scullery at the back of the shop had an old stone sink and an ancient gas stove, it was not a place where she fancied cooking her meals. Nor, at the moment, did she have time for cooking.

One afternoon, while she was stripping the shop walls, preparatory to repapering them, a woman who looked about sixty peered through the open door.

'My word! You have had a purge. Is Mr Beccles about?'

Jane descended the stepladder. 'He's having a nap in the back room. Who shall I say is calling?'

'Oh, don't disturb the dear man. I'm Rosamund Farnham. I've been a customer of his for years. I collect a number of things, most of which are very hard to come by at affordable prices these days. You must be the young woman who has come to live with him.'

'Jane Taunton. How do you do?'

Hector had spoken of Mrs Farnham. She had encouraged her children to spend their pocket money at his shop in the days when he had been able to keep a tray filled with objects at prices they could afford. Now her children were grown up and gone and she came in less often, but if he had anything of interest to her he put it aside.

'You collect Staffordshire blue, tortoiseshell boxes, Paisley shawls and foot-stools... is that correct?' said Jane, when they had shaken hands.

Mrs Farnham nodded and smiled. 'How clever of you to have me pigeon-holed already. I wonder if my information about you is equally accurate? I've heard that you were a top-flight secretary in London but have given it up to come and help Mr Beccles.'

'I don't know about "top flight"...where did you hear that?'

Mrs Farnham glanced at the door to the back room and lowered her voice slightly. 'From a friend of mine...Colonel Fontenay. I believe you're a friend of his son. Unfortunately, as I expect you know, dear old Mr B and the Fontenays don't see eye to eye. A pity, but there it is.' She changed the subject by asking, 'What are you going to do with the walls when you've finished stripping them?'

Presently they were joined by Hector and the three of them had a cup of tea together.

Before she left Mrs Farnham said to Jane, 'When you're not so busy, you must come and see my magpie's hoard.'

Jane made a polite response and thought no more about the invitation until a week later when she received a note asking her to 'an informal kitchen supper with a few young people I think you would enjoy meeting'. The note asked her to confirm by telephone that she was free on the proposed night.

When she rang up to accept, Mrs Farnham said, 'Good, that's splendid. As my house can be hard to find the first time, I've asked Margaret Poole to pick you up. She has to pass through Long Goosebeck to get here. Margaret's a farm secretary...a very capable girl whom I think you'll find a useful contact.'

'I'm not certain what to wear to a country supper party, Mrs Farnham.'

'Oh, anything...jeans...a skirt...whatever you feel comfortable in,' her hostess said vaguely.

* * *

Jane arrived at the party in a flowered cotton skirt which had once been a dress belonging to her sister.

With it she wore an embroidered white lawn blouse, made in India and bought from a street-market stall in London. A plain violet scarf to pick up the sprigs of violet in the skirt was knotted around her waist and she was wearing a pair of simple Brazilian leather sandals marked down at the end of last summer in one of the many shops selling inexpensive shoes in Oxford Street.

Several cars were already parked in front of Mrs Farnham's house when she arrived with Margaret, and it wasn't long before she was being introduced to their owners, a friendly group of young married couples who, it appeared, had grown up with their hostess's children.

Jane was sipping a glass of white wine and chatting to two of the wives, both of whom had worked in London at an earlier stage of their lives, when some more guests arrived. One of them was Adam Fontenay.

Although Mrs Farnham had mentioned knowing the Fontenays, somehow it had not occurred to Jane that Adam might be here tonight. The pre-dinner drinks were being served in a large conservatory built on to the back of the house. As soon as she saw him coming in, her relaxed mood changed to a state of uneasy tension.

At first she assumed he was escorting one of the young women who had entered a few steps ahead of him. But then it became clear that they had come with the men bringing up the rear and that Adam was on his own. She wondered, with a sinking feeling, if Mrs Farnham's party plan was for her to be, so to speak, Adam's partner.

'Hello, Adam. You're looking tanned for someone who works in London,' said one of the wives standing beside Jane as he came over to speak to them. 'But you only need one fine weekend to turn you as brown as a gypsy, don't you? It takes me ages to work up a decent tan. Jane, this is Adam Fontenay.'

Before she could complete the introduction, he said, 'Jane and I have met before, Lyn...several times. Hello, Jane.'

He smiled at her before turning to greet the young woman on the other side of her. 'Hello, Charlotte.' This time he bent to brush a light social kiss on Charlotte's uplifted cheek before moving on to greet some other people.

Obviously he was on closer terms with her than with Lyn, but that she might have once been one of his girl-friends was only conjecture on Jane's part. Neither of them asked where she had met him. They continued talking about clothes and she tried to pay attention and not think about the tall figure in pale blue Levis and a white Lacoste shirt whose presence she found so disturbing.

Presently Mrs Farnham summoned her guests—about fourteen in all—to supper in a large homely kitchen where the fitments consisted of four or five old-fashioned dressers ranged side by side along the walls, their shelves and hooks crowded with old dishes, jugs and mugs.

Two large tables, one spread with a gingham cloth and the other with rush mats on its waxed oak surface, were placed end to end. The first names of all the guests had been written with a thick-tipped red fibre pen on the slips of card on top of the paper napkins. Jane found that she was sitting next to a man called Jon whom she had not yet met. Her place was next to the foot of the table and that place had been allotted to Adam with someone called Liz on the other side of him, opposite Jane.

She was bracing herself for at least an hour, probably two, of unavoidable proximity, when her other neighbour spotted his place card, introduced himself and drew out her chair for her.

They were both sitting down, making small talk, when Adam came to his place, although he did not sit down until Liz had arrived and he had attended to seating her.

Like Jon, she introduced herself to Jane, explaining that she was the partner of the man in the yellow shirt at the other table.

She was a vivacious personality who dominated the conversation throughout the first course, a delicious cold, creamy, orange and carrot soup decorated with a dark red nasturtium flower.

Knowing that nasturtiums could be used in salads, Jane assumed the flower was intended to be eaten and then was embarrassed when everyone else seemed to be putting theirs aside. The only other person near her to eat the petals was Adam and she wondered if he had done so only out of consideration for her feelings. If he had, it was a gesture which did not tie in with what she had been told about him by Hector and Dick.

He did not speak directly to her until they came back from helping themselves to the main course, a selection of cold meats and salads set out at the far end of the room.

'Ros tells me the shop will be unrecognisable by the time you've finished with it,' he said.

The smile which accompanied this remark was the one she had seen many times during their first evening together and, as it had then, it sent a flutter of excitement and pleasure through her.

She said lightly, 'I'm enjoying refurbishing the place... the shop and the living quarters. Even the yard at the back has possibilities.'

'I'm sure it has, and Ros says you have excellent taste.'

'What a nice compliment... especially as Mrs Farnham's own taste is so good,' said Jane, looking at the nearest dresser with its motley collection of china, very few pieces matching but every one pleasing to the eye.

Adam said, 'She was my mother's closest friend. They met at an auction soon after my parents came here. They both had their eye on a very fine early Vic dolls' house.'

'Did someone else beat them to it?'

'No, Ros got it... and has it still. Being, at the time, a more experienced auction-goer than my mother, she knew that most people set their limit at a round figure which in those days might have been five shillings, ten shillings, a pound, a fiver and so on. Ros always set her limit a little above what she thought the top bid would be. My mother stopped at four pounds and Ros got the house for half a crown more... twelve and a half pence in today's currency.'

'I can understand two unsuccessful bidders commiserating with each other after losing something to a third party, but that doesn't sound like a promising beginning for a friendship,' said Jane.

'Part of the reason Ros wanted the house was because it was larger than the one she already had. Seeing my mother's disappointment, she asked if she'd like to have the smaller house, free. So Mother had Laburnum Villa which was the right size for someone starting to collect miniatures, and Ros was able to spread her already large collection in the ten rooms of Strawberry Hall. After supper I'll take you up to the playroom to see it.'

She was not sure she wanted to be taken to the playroom. Even here, safely surrounded by twelve other people, she was disturbingly conscious of the swell of a powerful muscle at the point where the sleeve of his shirt ended, exposing a long suntanned arm. Hidden under the table, perhaps only centimetres from her left knee, was his denim-clad right knee. If she felt this strong physical awareness of him down here in the kitchen, she knew it would be doubly potent in a distant part of the house, far from the chatter and laughter going on around them.

Without responding to his suggestion, she said to Liz, 'Did you have a dolls' house as a child?'

Liz shook her head. 'I was a tomboy...much preferred climbing trees and netting sticklebacks to playing with girls' toys. My ambition was to have a pony. You were keen on sailing, weren't you, Adam?'

To Jane's relief this remark led to a general conversation about sailing and her tête-à-tête with Adam was over, at least for the time being.

Nevertheless each time he topped up her wine glass—the men had been asked to help themselves and keep the women's glasses replenished—she found her eyes drawn to his hand, to the long shapely fingers which had once clamped on her shoulders.

Adam himself drank very little, she noticed, no doubt because he was driving. She remembered the last meal they had eaten together, at Annabel's. What madness it had been, to pretend to be someone else. She found herself wishing that tonight was their first meeting, that the foolish masquerade in London had never happened. She couldn't bear to think that he might tell Rosamund Farnham and other people what she had done. But he wouldn't. Would he?

What kind of man was he? A breaker of hearts, as Dick claimed? A man who, as a boy, had knowingly taken advantage of the ignorance of a shop-minder to gain an object worth many times what he had paid for it?

When the empty plates were being collected by two of the guests, Rosamund announced that there were three puddings: chocolate mousse, lemon cheesecake and fruit salad. Rather than have everyone queuing at the serving table, she suggested that only the men should come, 'After asking the girl on your right which pud she would like.'

Adam looked at Jane, raising a questioning eyebrow.

'Fruit salad, please.'

He pushed back his chair but remained seated. 'The healthy choice. What about cream? Yes? No?'

'A little cream, please.'

'That's what I thought you'd say.' There was a glint of mockery in his grey eyes as if her choice amused him.

When he came back and she saw what he had chosen, Liz said laughingly, 'What a cruel beast you are, Adam. You know I'm a chocoholic. How unfair to sit gorging yourself on that sinfully rich mousse while Jane and I peck at fruit salad.'

'I doubt if Jane is a chocoholic. If she is, she's got her addiction well under control,' he answered, with an appraising glance at what he could see of her slim figure. 'As you have,' he added diplomatically, smiling at Liz.

'Yes, but it isn't easy.'

While the men had been fetching the sweet course, she had told Jane about the diet on which she was hoping to lose seven pounds before going on holiday.

Jane had done her best to look interested while inwardly still reacting to the way Adam had looked at her. It would have been unfair to accuse him of undressing her with his eyes. Yet something in his expression had made her flesh tingle, her pulse quicken.

As she had on the night they had dined together at Annabel's, she had felt he was strongly attracted to her, even though this evening, in a cheap blouse and cotton skirt, she had none of the superficial sophistication and allure she had had in London.

But *why* did he want her? That was the crucial question. When, long ago, Nick had looked at her like that, she hadn't questioned his motives. She had thought he was falling in love. As he had been . . . as she had.

Now, older and wiser, she knew there were numerous reasons why men desired women, and many of them had nothing to do with love. Years of listening to other women's confidences had taught her that most women's heartaches were caused by her sex's tendency to delude themselves, to believe what they wanted to believe.

She herself longed to be loved by a strong, tender, caring man. It would be dangerously easy to ascribe those qualities to Adam when someone whose emotions were not involved would quickly discern that in reality his assurance sprang from selfishness rather than strength.

As she began to eat the fruit he had fetched for her, she reminded herself that two people she liked didn't like him.

Mrs Farnham did like him, but no doubt her opinion must be coloured by the fact that he was the son of a close friend, which naturally would predispose her to think well of him. Also she was a woman and therefore not immune to his charm. In general men were the best judges of other men, and neither Hector nor Dick had a good word to say for him.

Having aired her own holiday plans, Liz asked Adam where he was going.

'I'm not. Airports during the tourist season are my idea of hell,' was his reply.

'You can say that now, but when you have a family you won't be able to go except in the school holidays,' she pointed out.

'When that time comes I shall do what my parents did... head in the opposite direction from the crowds.'

So a wife and family were on his agenda, thought Jane. But not, by the sound of it, in the foreseeable future.

He turned to her. 'Drinking Bovril in the shelter of a wind-break typifies my childhood holidays. We went to the Hebrides, the Channel Islands and sometimes to Normandy and Brittany. I think we had a lot more fun collecting shells and digging complicated waterways between tides than the people who lie on the beaches of southern Europe, working up a tan. What sort of holidays did you have?'

'Stay-at-home holidays with some day trips to London to see famous places or visit museums. My father was overseas and the aunt who looked after my sister and me in the holidays couldn't afford to go away. I've never been abroad.'

'Haven't you? Never?' Liz exclaimed in astonishment. 'But surely you could have gone since you've been grown up? Aren't you interested in other countries?'

Before Jane could answer, Adam said crisply, 'My dear Liz, going to a foreign resort for a couple of weeks doesn't necessarily indicate an interest in the country. You've been to Greece several times. Do you know ten words of the language? Can you tell me five interesting things about the Parthenon?'

She looked disconcerted. As well she might, thought Jane. Liz had meant no harm by her comment. Perhaps it had been a bit tactless, but had it deserved Adam's scathing riposte?

'Well . . . no, I can't,' Liz admitted. 'But we didn't go to Athens. We went to the islands and we didn't need to speak the language. The waiters and shop-keepers all spoke some English.'

'Which relieved you of the bother of learning to say "please" and "thank you" and "good morning" in their language.'

His tone had a cutting edge which made Liz flush.

Jane said quickly, 'Of the countries you've been to, Liz, which do you like best?'

There was an awkward pause of a few seconds before Liz answered, 'Actually I like America better than anywhere in Europe. Not just because they speak English——' flicking a peeved glance at Adam '—but because, in Florida for instance, they not only have wonderful beaches but the other facilities are better. It depends what you enjoy. I'm not all that keen on museums and old churches. Adam will raise his eyebrows, but I'd rather browse round a shopping mall.'

Adam didn't raise his eyebrows but he gave a slight shrug and said pleasantly, 'As you say, everyone to their taste. My favourite country is Italy but I think my father is right. The best time to travel is over. We live in the age of tourism, which isn't the same thing.'

Jane was about to ask if the prospect of space travel appealed to him when Liz said to her, 'If you've never been abroad, where have you been going for holidays?'

'To my married sister in the country. While I was working in London, I enjoyed staying in a village and it gave my sister a chance to go shopping on her own, without the children. Don't you think the important thing about a holiday is that it should be a complete change from one's everyday life?'

This remark, overheard by the man on her right who, earlier, had been talking to his other neighbour, prompted him to tell them about a group holiday for amateur photographers he had been on the year before.

The meal ended with coffee or herb tea. Jane thought that by now Adam had probably forgotten about showing her their hostess's dolls' house. She would have liked to see it but not at the price of another tête-à-tête.

She was still puzzled by his sharpness with Liz. Part of her wanted to believe that he had been crushing to Liz because he felt her remark had been a put-down—even if not intentional—for Jane.

But common sense told her that his caustic response might have had nothing to do with her. Its only significance might be that he was not a man to suffer fools gladly and Liz's assumption that everyone must have been abroad was rather foolish.

Dishes of home-made fudge were passed round with the coffee and presently Rosamund Farnham circled the table, refilling people's coffee-cups.

Adam declined a second cup. 'May I take Jane up to the playroom to have a look at Strawberry Hall?'

'Of course, my dear,' she said, giving his shoulder an affectionate pat before passing on.

The Chinese teapot containing the herb tea was being brought round by someone else. Ignoring the possibility that Jane might have liked another cup, he pushed back his chair and rose. An instant later he was grasping the back of her chair, waiting for her to stand up. She had no option but to go with him.

The first and second floors were reached by a wide Turkey-carpeted staircase rising to spacious landings furnished with chairs and side-tables supporting glass cases of stuffed birds and bouquets of flowers made of shells protected by glass domes.

But the narrower flight of bare stairs to the topmost floor was through a door which Adam closed behind him.

'I'll lead the way now, shall I?' he said, as she hesitated, noting how the solid mahogany door cut off the sound of the party going on downstairs.

'This part of the house was where the maids slept up to the Second World War,' he continued, his footsteps on the unpolished wood making less noise and vibration than might have been expected considering his size. In spite of his height and breadth of shoulder, he was not a heavy-footed man. 'They've always been playrooms in my time... and still are, when Ros's grandchildren come to stay.'

Jane wondered if Ros would have liked to have him for a son-in-law. If her daughters were as nice as their mother, it seemed surprising he hadn't fallen for one of them.

Several doors led off the top landing. Opening one, Adam said, 'This largest attic was a dormitory for the housemaids. When Ros and her husband inherited the house, he built this layout for his collection of model trains which we were allowed to play with under his supervision.'

'It must be worth a lot of money now,' said Jane, looking at the complex network of lines, stations, level crossings, tunnels and sidings filled with miniature steam engines, coaches and freight waggons, all protected from dust by a large sheet of transparent plastic.

'It is. Not long ago Crowthorne's sold a 1909 station by Märklin, one of the famous German toy-train makers, for twenty-four thousand pounds, even though it had been restored and repainted. Pressed tinplate toys of the kind given as Christmas presents between 1880 and 1960 have shot up in value. This layout wouldn't fetch that sort of money, but it's a valuable collection. Not that Ros wants to sell. She intends to keep it for her grandsons.'

He turned to open another door. 'In this room the girls had a farm and a riding stable. The pieces are all stored away in boxes but you can see where the farm buildings stood.'

From the threshold of this smaller attic, she saw that the floorboards had been painted grass-green. To this had been added grey roads and paths with white cattle grids, a meandering blue river, a pond and yellow patches representing corn fields.

'It must be fun growing up in a large house, and presumably yours is even larger?'

'Yes, but I didn't have the run of the attics. They were used for storage. We have never used more than a small part of the house to live in. The rest of it looks like a private house but is actually a shop.'

He moved on to open a third room and, as he ushered her into it, Jane saw that it housed a collection which reminded her of the Museum of Childhood at Bethnal Green, an otherwise rather unlovely part of outer London to which she had gone with Aunt Dee.

A rocking horse, a doll-sized perambulator, clockwork animals, a toy butcher's shop hung with miniature sides of beef; the attic contained a profusion of Victorian and Edwardian children's treasures. But the *pièce de résistance* was the large double-fronted dolls' house standing on a low table so that its interior would be at a convenient level for little girls.

When Adam folded back the façade, hinged on both sides, she gave a gasp of delight.

'How Apple would *love* this! Perhaps I can bring her to see it when she comes to stay with me.'

'Apple? Who is Apple?'

'My... my god-daughter.'

She felt hot blood flooding her face in a burning blush. To hide it, she bent to peer into the basement kitchen where a cook in a print dress and starched white pinafore was making pastry with a disproportionately large rolling pin which Jane guessed must be a needle-case.

'I'm sure Ros would be delighted for her to see it. And you must bring her to see my mother's dolls' house. Which reminds me, I have a proposition to put to you. May I run you home?'

CHAPTER FIVE

HER cheeks still hot, Jane said, 'I came with Margaret Poole. I don't think it would be polite to leave with someone else.'

'Maggie won't mind. I'll explain that I want to talk to you.'

'Can't we talk here?'

'Not now, while you're looking at the dolls' house. I want your undivided attention.'

He sat down in an old club-shaped chair with a shabby cretonne cover, evidently prepared to wait while she studied the dolls' house in detail.

There was a rug on the floor in front of Strawberry Hall and Jane sank on to her knees, a more comfortable position for gazing into the rooms than viewing them from a bending posture.

In other circumstances she would have enjoyed a leisurely inspection of the drawing-room, the bedrooms, the nursery where a portly nanny with grey wool hair was bathing a celluloid baby.

But at present her mind was in too much confusion to concentrate on anything fully. Her eyes registered details such as the scarlet macaw on its perch in the hall and china-faced mistress of the house knitting with dressmaker's pins, but she was still regretting her unguarded exclamation when first he had opened the house for her.

She had lied to him once and regretted it. Now she had told him a half-truth and felt as miserable about it as if she had lied to him again.

Footsteps on the staircase signalled that someone was coming to join them. It was Rosamund Farnham.

'Don't get up, Adam. I just came to tell Jane that Margaret has had to leave early. Her mother's cat has been clawed by a neighbour's tom and Mrs Poole wants Margaret to hurry home to minister to it. Really that woman is a pain in the neck. Possessive... helpless... unbelievably selfish. I don't know how Margaret stands it. Her mother has already put the kibosh on two budding romances. I don't think poor Margaret will ever get away from her.'

'She doesn't have to put up with her mother's selfishness,' Adam said drily. 'If she had a bit more gumption, she'd have told Mrs Poole to deal with the cat's wounds herself.'

'Easier said than done, my dear. Margaret's been under her mother's thumb all her life. I doubt if she'll ever rebel. She was worried about leaving Jane in the lurch but I said you would run her back.'

'With pleasure. Excuse me: I want to have a word with the Strattons before they leave.'

Taking his place in the armchair, Mrs Farnham said, 'The Strattons have an elderly baby-sitter who won't stay after eleven so they're always the first to leave.'

She leaned forward and began to tell Jane about some of the things in the house; where she had found them and how, often, they had cost only a few pence in the days when her children were small and a pound went a long way.

When, half an hour later, they went downstairs, people began to depart. Tomorrow was Saturday and although most of those present did not have to go to work they had the family obligations of couples with children, and parents and in-laws living locally. Even Liz, though not married, was paired.

The only unattached women were Margaret, who seemed bound to her mother, and Jane herself, whose future was uncertain. Would the time ever come when she had a partner? she wondered, as she watched those who had saying goodnight.

At that moment Adam came to where she was standing. 'Time to go, I think, don't you?'

'What about the washing-up? Oughtn't we to help with that first?'

'Ros has a large dishwasher. It's already been loaded. Everything is under control.'

When their turn came to say goodnight, Jane said, 'It's been a lovely evening, Mrs Farnham. Thank you so much for inviting me.'

'Oh, do call me Ros,' said her hostess. 'You must come again...soon.' She surprised Jane by leaning forward and kissing her cheek. 'I was watching you during supper...thinking how charming you looked in that summery blouse and what a good listener you are. The world is full of chatterers, but people who really listen are rather rare...aren't they, Adam?'

Her praise was as unexpected as her kiss, but Jane had a guilty feeling that when she might have appeared to be listening intently she had actually been thinking about the tall man beside her, with whom she was soon to be closeted even more privately than during their visit to the attics.

'How long has Ros been a widow?' she asked, as they fastened their seatbelts.

'About fifteen years. Everyone liked Miles but he wasn't much use as a husband...kept losing what money they had in hare-brained schemes to get rich, and he drank more than was good for him. He used to begrudge Ros spending money on her collections, but in fact she made more than she spent. She has an excellent eye and sometimes made hefty profits on things sold by Crowthorne's at auction. But, according to my parents, she and Miles were happy in spite of the money worries.'

When Jane had arrived with Margaret, they had entered the drive by a right turn and, as they paused in the gateway, she expected Adam to turn left. Instead he turned in the opposite direction, evidently intending to deliver her to Goosebeck by a different route.

'What is it you want to talk to me about?' she prompted, when they had been driving for some minutes in silence.

'My father is getting on. He won't hear of retiring yet, but certain aspects of the business are too much for him. He needs a reliable assistant. I wondered if you would be interested?'

'But I have a job...looking after Hector and getting his business going again. I thought when your father did retire, you would be taking over. Why not work with him now?'

'Because I have just been offered a seat on Crowthorne's board at twice my present salary and I've accepted it,' he answered. 'The future of businesses such as my father's is very uncertain, Jane. Already fine pieces are scarce and in ten years' time, or sooner, they may be unobtainable at prices his kind of customers can afford to pay. That applies at all levels of the antiques trade. I don't think you will be able to revive old Beccles' business. It's been moribund for some time.'

'It's in a bad way—yes. But I think I can pull it round. It's worth trying.'

'Local gossip has it that the old boy's in bad shape…in fact seriously ill.'

'Yes, he is,' she agreed. 'Which is why I couldn't possibly desert him.'

'I wasn't suggesting that you should, merely that instead of attempting to carry on the business after he dies you might think about working with my father. He's almost as old as Beccles but his health is good and, as both his father and grandfather lived to be ninety-something, there's a good chance Dad will as well.'

'Have you discussed this with him?'

'No, I thought I'd sound you out first.'

'What makes you think I would suit him?' she asked. Adding, 'If I were free?'

'If you were a senior secretary in London, as I hear you were, and if, single-handed, you've transformed that chaotic shop into a neat and clean one, you must be an unusually capable person. Added to which, as Ros said when we were leaving, you're very easy on the eye and you wouldn't show you were bored if my father started reminiscing, as he's rather prone to these days.'

He made her sound a paragon, yet he knew she was not. He had had direct experience of the flaws in her character.

'Think it over, Jane,' he went on. 'Don't dismiss it out of hand. There are a great many pitfalls involved in running a business. Both my parents have often said that, had they known how hard it would be at times to keep going, they would never have set up as dealers. And they started out in the days when stock was abundant. It was customers who were scarce then.'

She said, 'If I were a free agent... if I were looking for a job, I should like to work for your father... if he found me an acceptable assistant. But Hector may live for some time. I hope he does. I've become rather fond of him... although I know you dislike him and he dislikes you.'

She hoped that this remark would lead Adam to explain his side of the Beccles-Fontenay feud, but he didn't pick up the cue. A few moments later he braked and turned the car off the narrow by-road, which she had assumed was a short-cut, to drive down an untarred lane with the shimmer of moonlit water at the end of it.

'I used to come here to fish as a small boy,' he said. 'It's a nice spot for picnics which you may not have discovered yet.'

Near the water's edge, the lane widened into a grassy clearing, large enough for half a dozen cars to park. But there were no other cars there now, at ten minutes to midnight.

'There's a path all the way round the lake. I thought you might like to stretch your legs before turning in,' he said, as he switched off the headlights and the engine.

It was certainly a perfect night for a stroll. The sky was clear, the moon almost full. Had Dick been her companion, Jane would have had no qualms as he walked round the car to open the passenger's door for her. But Dick would have asked beforehand if she thought it was a good idea. Adam took her acquiescence for granted, and a stroll in the moonlight with him was fraught with possibilities which made her insides clench with apprehension.

She might, the first time he met her, have looked like a sophisticate, and certainly she was at an age when people would conclude she had the aplomb to cope with most situations. But in fact she hadn't. Life had taught her very little about handling men like Adam.

She could cope with Dick because he was the kind of man who would never do anything without being sure of his ground. But Adam was an altogether bolder, more assured personality. It would never cross his mind that he was dealing with someone whose experience of life and men had been, in some ways, as restricted as that of his mother's generation.

'I imagine you've been too busy to do much exploring,' he said, as she stepped out of the car.

'Yes.' Would he recognise the husky monosyllable as a sign of nervousness? She doubted it.

Maybe she should walk to the water's edge, admire the view and then announce regretfully but firmly that it was too late for a walk. Hector might wake and be worried if he found her out after midnight.

But before she could turn thought into action, Adam took her lightly by the hand. 'This way.'

The physical contact didn't last long because the path round the lake was not wide enough for two people to walk side by side unless they were lovers, moving hip against hip, their arms around each other's waists. Where the path began, he fell back half a pace, walking close enough to rest a hand on her shoulder if he chose.

But he kept his hands to himself and she told herself hopefully that she might be jumping to conclusions. A little night air and exercise could be all he had in mind.

Her throat slightly less constricted, she said, 'Is this a natural lake? Somebody told me there were some old gravel workings which had been flooded in this area.'

'There are, but this isn't one of them. The mere has been here for centuries. I learnt sail-boarding and skin-diving here. Ros's elder son was crazy about water sports in his bachelor days and his brother and I picked up his enthusiasm. Are you comfortable in the water, Jane?'

'I know how to swim. I haven't had a lot of practice.'

'If the warm weather holds, I'll organise a weekend beach party.'

The path had come to a clearing, a grassy space among the surrounding trees and thickets of blackberry bushes. A light breeze rustled the rushes growing on both sides of an old, dilapidated diving platform.

As Jane paused to look round, Adam turned her to face him.

'I've been wanting to do this since the first time I saw you,' he said. And took her face between his hands before bending his head to kiss her gently on the lips.

It was so long, so many years since she had felt a man's mouth moving softly against hers. Even though she had half expected this to happen, the tenderness of it came as a shock. It was not the kind of kiss she had expected from him.

At first she could not respond, could only stand with closed eyes submitting to an almost forgotten sensation while her heart beat in slow, nervous thumps.

And then, all at once, while her mind was still grappling with the situation, instinct took over and she found her lips moving in response.

With a slow and gentle stroking motion Adam's hands moved from her cheeks and passed lightly over her hair, one to cup the back of her head, the other to move caressingly from her shoulders to her waist.

'Mmm...' The sound came from deep in his throat: a wordless murmur of satisfaction and pleasure as his arm enfolded and drew her closer.

She had forgotten how good it felt to be pressed to a taller, stronger body. Without knowing how they had come there, she found her hands exploring his broad, hard shoulders, enjoying their latent strength. She felt herself relaxing, dormant emotions reviving.

It was a disappointment when, suddenly, he stopped kissing her.

'I think I had better take you home.' His voice was as husky as hers had been earlier, but from a different cause.

In the pause that followed she knew with certainty that what he would have liked to do was to strip off his clothes, and hers, and make love to her. And that was what she wanted too. Every cell, every nerve in her body demanded to rediscover the delights she had known once before and now longed to experience again in the arms of this tall, dark-haired man.

Then Adam released his hold and stepped away and she knew it would have been madness to let him make love to her but that, if he had tried, she might not have been able to stop him.

They didn't speak on the way back to the car. Jane wondered if Adam had taken her to that secluded spot with the intention of making love to her and for some reason changed his mind. Yet somehow it didn't seem likely.

When the car was back on the road, he said, 'Tomorrow I'm flying to New York. I'll be away for two weeks. When I come back, will you have dinner with me?'

His voice was under control; so much so that she wondered if it had been wishful thinking to suppose that he had been close to losing command of his emotions.

'Thank you... I'd like to. Are you going to New York on business?'

He explained the purpose of his visit which, after a few days in New York, was going to take him to several American cities.

As he talked, Jane wondered if he would kiss her again when they said goodnight. Merely thinking about it made her tremble with nervous anticipation. She knew this reaction was absurd for a woman of her age. But in terms of experience she was not like most women in their late twenties who, even when single, had usually had several close relationships with men.

She had known only one, and he hadn't been a man of the world but a boy pretending to be more experienced than he was. They had both been babes in the wood compared with the sophisticated man beside her. She wondered who Adam's first girl had been, and if he remembered her clearly or only dimly as the first of a long succession of women he had made love to. Perhaps she had not been a girl but a woman older than himself, their relationship based on mutual physical satisfaction but little or no deep emotional involvement. Perhaps his relationships with women were always like that.

The thought displeased Jane. She didn't want to believe it. But common sense told her it was a strong possibility. If a man had not found a woman he wanted to marry by the time he was Adam's age, it might be because he was not the marrying kind, preferring to play the field.

Adam didn't kiss her goodnight. Having seen her to the door of the shop and unlocked it for her, he touched her cheek with his knuckles and said, 'Take care of yourself till I get back.'

Inwardly tense, she said, 'Thank you for bringing me home.'

'It was the best part of the evening. Goodnight.'

He turned and walked back to the car.

While Adam was in America, Dick invited Jane to a drinks party at his parents' house.

'Mum will be doing the catering because she enjoys it, but it's my party for my friends,' he explained. 'Dad and Mum don't entertain much themselves, although she's a good cook, especially with cakes and fancy stuff. Sally...my wife...used to love giving parties. She'd cook a load of pasta and knock up some sauce and a salad, and that would be it. No fuss, no bother, and everyone just as happy with spaghetti bolognese or bangers and mash as something which costs a lot and takes hours to prepare. But Mum says she likes all that fiddling with vol-au-vents and what-have-you. So if it makes her happy...' He gave a good-humoured shrug.

The day before the party Jane became the owner of a second-hand car supplied by the village garage. So she was able to drive to the Osbornes' house instead of going on her bicycle or having Dick fetch her.

The spread prepared by his mother was set out in the dining-room of a house which surprised Jane by having none of the choice antiques she had expected to find in an auctioneer's home.

Everything in the house was of excellent quality but she knew as soon as she entered the hall that she and Dick's mother were not on the same wavelength. Jane could never have lived with Mrs Osborne's choice of carpet and curtains and, while most people did some extra tidying and cleaning before giving a party, she sensed that his mother might be excessively house-proud.

After Dick had introduced them, her hostess showed Jane the way to an immaculate guest bedroom. But although she knew from the cars in the drive and the sound of voices from a sitting-room that she was not the first comer, there were no coats, shawls or other wraps on either of the twin beds. As Jane slipped off the jacket she was wearing over her dress, Mrs Osborne took it from her and put it on a hanger in the wardrobe.

No doubt it was better for the guests' things to be hung up than to lie in a heap for several hours, but it did hint at obsessive tidiness, thought Jane as they exchanged polite nothings.

'Dick tells me you were a secretary in London. You must find country life very quiet, don't you?' said Mrs Osborne.

'I prefer it. I was never a town mouse,' Jane said with a smile, conscious that her hostess was discreetly scrutinising the dress her guest was wearing, perhaps trying to put a label and a price on it.

Adam's colleagues in Crowthorne's antique clothes department would have recognised instantly that it was a pre-war model. Olivia Chichester had bought it for three guineas—the Thirties equivalent of three pounds fifteen pence but worth far more at a time when the average working-class wage was fifty shillings a week—

from a shop called Marshall and Snelgrove, long since disappeared from the list of London's department stores.

A typical 'afternoon frock' of its period, with a hip-hugging skirt with a swirl of godets at knee-level and a jabot neckline, the dress was made of soft silk georgette patterned with small smudgy blobs of yellow and white on a dark blue ground. It had the finishing touches—fabric-covered press-studs, hand-made silk eyes for the hooks, a bias-bound and hand-sewn hem—characteristic of even medium price clothes of the period.

What Mrs Osborne thought of it, Jane couldn't tell, but it made her feel good to wear it. Inheriting Mrs Chichester's wardrobe had taught her that anything exquisitely made invested its wearer with extraordinary self-confidence, or at least it had that effect on her. Or perhaps her present state of mind had less to do with the dress than with living in the country, doing work she enjoyed, and beginning to make friends.

At any rate she was much less conscious of being an outsider than she had been the night she went to Crowthorne's exhibition and met Adam.

'I suppose your grandson is in bed?' she said.

Mrs Osborne nodded. 'I don't agree with the modern idea of letting children stay up till all hours. Tommy has his bath at six-thirty, sharp. It's what he's used to and what's good for him. He may not be asleep yet, but he knows better than to come down once he's been tucked in and had his goodnight kiss. He's a good little chap, no trouble...the image of my late daughter-in-law. A lovely girl, she was.'

'Yes, Dick has told me about her...a dreadful tragedy for all of you,' said Jane.

'It was...especially for him. They were made for each other...ideally suited. Dick hides his feelings for the boy's sake. But he hasn't got over it. I don't know that he ever will.'

Message received and understood, thought Jane, as they left the bedroom. But she didn't resent it. It was natural for Mrs Osborne to be wary of single women who might have designs on her son. A man in his situation was particularly vulnerable to designing females and there were still plenty of women who, although not really attracted, would see him as a comfortable meal ticket.

Dick was hovering in the hall. 'Hello, Jane. That's a pretty dress. Sorry I wasn't around when you arrived. I was keeping an eye out for your car but was temporarily hog-tied by someone who never draws a breath. Before we go into the lounge, would you like to pop up and say hello to Tommy?'

As his mother was still standing by, Jane said, 'I'd like to meet him, Dick, but is it a good idea to take a stranger up now when he's in bed? He's probably half asleep.'

'Not yet, he won't be. Come on.'

Jane hesitated. 'What do you think, Mrs Osborne?'

His mother shrugged her plump shoulders. 'He's Dick's child. I'm only his granny.'

'The best there is, according to your grandson,' Dick said diplomatically. 'We'll be down in two ticks, Mum.'

The child's room was at the end of a thickly carpeted passage. When Dick opened the bedroom door, the little boy sat up expectantly, obviously wide awake.

'This is Miss Taunton,' said his father.

'Hello, Tommy.' Jane moved to the bedside and held out her hand to him, smiling.

Obviously well schooled in politeness, he put his small hand into hers and said formally, 'How do you do?'

The freshly bathed glow of his skin, the friendly curiosity in his eyes reminded her of her sister's children, especially Apple.

'Did you help with the preparations for Daddy's party?' she asked.

'A bit. I counted out the serviettes and Granny let me lick the spoon she mixed the cake with... after she'd finished with it,' he added. 'Are you the lady who tidied up Mr Beccles?'

'I've helped him to spring-clean his shop, yes.'

'I thought it looked an interesting shop,' the little boy told her. 'But Granny wouldn't go there. She said it was a hive of germs.'

Jane laughed. 'Perhaps it was, but there are no germs now, so next time you and your granny are passing I hope you'll come and say hello to me. Now I'd better say goodbye and go down or she will be cross with me for disturbing you. Goodnight, Tommy. Sleep tight.'

'Night-night, old chap.' Dick bent to kiss the child's cheek and then, as the boy lay down, smoothed the bedclothes under his chin.

'What very nice manners he has,' she said, as they went down the stairs. 'It can be a pain talking to children who haven't been taught to respond in a civilised way.'

'That's what Sally used to say. She trained him to shake hands properly and have something to say for himself.' Dick chuckled. 'Although, with kids of his age, that can sometimes lead to bricks being dropped, as it did just now.'

'A very small, unimportant brick. Your mother was right. Cousin Hector's place was pretty filthy before I arrived.'

Lowering his voice, he said, 'Mum is a bit of a fanatic, the more so as she gets older. I think there are going to be clashes before too much longer. Three generations under one roof nearly always raises problems. Small boys are naturally scruffy and clumsy and this house is designed to suit an elderly couple. Mum wouldn't take it lightly if he accidentally broke one of her treasured pieces of Lladro.'

He gestured towards a large china cabinet opposite the front door.

'They're not all safely behind glass. Several of her favourite pieces are on show in the lounge. We started off by buying a piece as a present for her when we were on our honeymoon in Spain. Now you can get Lladro in England and Dad gives her a piece every birthday and Christmas.'

At this point the door chimes sounded and he opened the door to some more guests, a young married couple who had brought a bottle wrapped in gift paper with them.

'You know where to put your coat, Pauli,' said Dick, when he had introduced them as Mark and Pauline East. 'It's time you had a glass in your hand, Jane. What can I get you. A gin and tonic? Wine? Martini?'

'Wine, please.'

Flanked by the two men, Jane entered the Osbornes' lounge where half a dozen people were grouped in the centre of the room discussing, she gathered, a television serial.

'Revivers first. Introductions second,' said Dick, leaving her with Mark, while he went to get drinks for them.

Grasping what the others were discussing, Mark said, 'Not having a video, we don't watch the serials. It's frustrating to miss an instalment that clashes with a party. Pauline's on at me to buy a video, but there's not a lot we'd record if we had one. Do you have one?'

Jane shook her head. 'I live with an elderly relation who doesn't approve of TV. According to him, TV programmes about antiques have ruined the trade.'

'Why's that?'

'First by making collecting fashionable so that too many people are chasing too few antiques—which encourages faking—and secondly by giving people an inflated idea of the value of old pieces. I'm not sure if he's right on either count, but I can't say I miss television. But then I've always preferred reading to viewing.'

They were joined by his wife who, overhearing this remark, said, 'We don't have the time for reading, do we, Mark? We're both working and two nights a week we go to evening classes. We lead a very full life.'

She slipped her hand through his arm and smiled up at him, but she did not share the smile with Jane. Indeed, when she looked at her again there was a hint of hostility in Pauline's eyes.

The possessive gesture combined with her unfriendly expression reminded Jane of overhearing some of the junior staff laughing about a similar reaction from one of the executive wives at the firm's annual dinner dance.

'And I wouldn't have her old man as a gift,' one of the typists had said with a giggle.

Jane had never been on the receiving end of wifely hostility herself and couldn't believe that Pauline saw her as a threat. Yet as the party progressed she was increasingly aware that although all the men were nice to her, the women were not. She was definitely getting the cold shoulder. None of them included her in the conversation and whenever she made a remark it was always the men who responded, never the women.

Partly because they succeeded in making her feel uncomfortable, she was the first to leave.

Dick saw her to her car. As she unlocked it, he said, 'Give me a ring when you get home, will you? Otherwise I shall wonder if you've got back all right.'

'It's only three miles.'

'All the same I'll feel happier knowing you're safely there. You're not dressed for changing a tyre, even if you could get the wheel off. If it's been locked on with a power tool, you might not be able to.'

'All right, I'll ring you,' she promised, settling herself in the driving seat, making sure her skirt was not in the way when Dick closed the door for her. 'Thank you for a very nice evening. Your mother's buffet was delicious.'

'The trouble is that, looking a knock-out in that dress, you made the others look dowdy and they didn't like it,' he said, bending to talk to her through the window.

'But this is a pre-war dress which my landlady in London gave me. Some of their outfits were far more fashionable,' she protested.

'But not as sexy as yours.'

Astonished by the comment—and also a bit disconcerted by the tone in which he made it—she said, 'I wouldn't call this a sexy dress. Quite the opposite.'

'A dress doesn't have to have a low neckline and a short skirt to be sexy,' he told her. 'Believe me, that's a very sexy dress and you look great in it.'

Jane was beginning to wonder if Dick had had slightly too much to drink. The unspoken message she was receiving from him was that if he hadn't had to return to his guests he would have got into the car with her and attempted some heavy necking.

She decided the best thing to do was to say politely, 'Thank you, and thanks again for the party. Goodnight, Dick.'

As she spoke she switched on the engine, but couldn't put the car in gear until he stepped away from it.

'I think you ought to have a cell-phone. Women drivers can't be too careful these days.'

'I'm not doing any long-distance driving and very little night driving.'

'There are crackpots everywhere these days . . . and you're a very attractive lady.'

Jane felt sure now that he had had one too many. 'I'll think about it. Goodnight, Dick.'

She moved the car gently forward.

Hector was awake when she got back. 'Make me a cup of tea, would you, Janie?' he said. He had taken to calling her Janie and she rather liked it. 'And I'll have a drop of whisky in it.'

While she waited for the kettle to boil, she cut some wholemeal bread and made a sandwich from a remnant of Brie and a slice of onion.

'Didn't they feed you?' said Hector, when she took up his tea.

'Yes, but it wasn't my kind of food. Lots of itsy-bitsy mouthfuls and splodges of tinned pâté.'

'I gave up going to that sort of do years ago. Put more than eight people in a room and you can't hear what anyone's saying. Meet anyone interesting?'

She shook her head. 'I enjoyed myself more at Mrs Farnham's party.'

'Well, you don't have to go there again... unless you fancy young Osborne.'

'I haven't known him very long.'

'Doesn't take long to know whether you fancy someone,' said Hector. 'Whether you'd suit in the long run... well, that's a different matter. You could do a lot worse, I reckon. He's a decent chap... never heard anything but good of him... good son... good husband... good prospects.'

'That being so, he can take his pick, and I can't see any reason why he should pick on me. I'm not in my first flush, Hector.'

'What does that matter? A young girl's no good to him. He needs a mother for his child and a wife who knows how to make him comfortable.'

She got up to refill his cup. 'I'm fully occupied making you comfortable.'

She spoke without thinking and regretted the remark when he said, 'For the time being... but not for much longer.'

'Oh, Hector...' Her eyes filled with tears. Impulsively she bent and put her lips to his cheek. 'I would like it to be for a long time. I'm so happy living here with you.'

He said gruffly, 'It's a pity you didn't come to me in the first place. But at least now you'll have a roof over your head and the business, such as it is. I'd like to have left you a nest egg . . . and would have done, if those thieving Fontenays hadn't stolen the Fabergé cat from me.'

CHAPTER SIX

THE day after the party, Jane bought a thank-you card she thought would appeal to Dick's mother and wrote an appreciative note about the buffet.

When a week passed without any word from him, she began to wonder if he was feeling embarrassed about his remarks at the car, or if his mother had said something to put him off her. Even men of his age could be influenced by their mothers' views and Dick was in a situation where it would be difficult for him to continue a friendship which his mother was strongly opposed to.

By the same token it was awkward for Jane to have a relationship with Adam when both he and his father were so bitterly disliked, and perhaps with good reason, by Hector.

Throughout the time Adam was out of the country, Jane was aware that her life lacked a quality it had when he was in England. For even though much of his time was spent in London, there was no telling when he might come home for a night between weekends. And the possibility of seeing him gave an exhilarating touch of suspense to her days; an element she missed when it wasn't there.

On the day Adam was due to fly in to London, she was working in the back yard when she heard Hector shouting for her to come to the telephone. Wondering if it could be Adam calling, she hurried into the house.

But it was Dick on the line.

'Are you free this evening?'

'Yes.'

'Would you like a run to the coast?'

'That sounds nice.'

'I'll pick you up at six-thirty.'

Evidently Dick had told Hector who was calling because, as soon as she rang off, the old man said, 'Made a date with him, have you?'

'Yes... for this evening. You don't mind, I hope?'

'Glad to see you having a good time. You've wasted enough of your life from what I can make out. No sense in wasting any more. Enjoy yourself. Squeeze every last drop of juice out of life.'

When she laughed, he said, 'What's the joke?'

'I was wondering how Dick would react if I asked for champagne to drink and chose something extravagant to eat. I think his face might fall a bit.'

'Try it and see what happens? If he penny-pinches now, when he's courting you, he won't be more generous later, that's a certainty.'

'He isn't courting me, Hector. We're just friends...two unattached people with certain things in common. Most of the time we talk about auctions and antiques, not personal matters.'

'I'm glad to hear it. Sweet nothings aren't enough to keep a conversation going for fifty years.'

Less than half an hour after Dick's call, he summoned her for the second time.

'Some girl from London,' he said. 'I didn't catch her name.'

Could it be someone from the firm she had worked for? Jane wondered. Or one of the other women who had lived in Mrs Chichester's house?

She took the receiver from him. 'Jane Taunton speaking.'

'Good afternoon, Miss Taunton. Mr Fontenay would like to speak to you. Just a moment, please.'

Fortunately Hector chose that moment to get up from his chair beside the telephone table. 'Sit yourself down. I'm going to the privy.' He still called it that although the old outside loo was now accessible from the house and modernised, with a handbasin and washing-machine in what had been a dingy scullery. Above it, the tiny third bedroom had been converted into a bathroom.

Jane took his place in the winged chair. Her heart had begun to thump as soon as the girl said Adam's name. Now, waiting to hear his voice, she found it difficult to breathe.

'Hello, Jane. How are you?'

'I—I'm fine. How are you? Was your trip successful?'

'Yes, but I'm glad to be back. There's nothing urgent on my desk so I'm taking a couple of days off. I'll be home by six at the latest. Will you have dinner with me?'

'I'm afraid I can't. I'm going out this evening.'

'What about tomorrow, then?'

'I don't think I ought to leave Hector alone two nights running. He... he may not be here for much longer.'

'I understand. How are you fixed for the weekend? Would Friday night be good for you?'

'Friday would be fine. I'm looking forward to hearing about your trip.'

'Until Friday, then.' Without discussing where they would meet or what time, he rang off.

When Hector came back he didn't ask who had telephoned because as he was passing through the kitchen he had one of his dizzy spells and had to be helped to bed. Suddenly he looked so ill that, despite his protests, Jane called the doctor.

By the following weekend Hector was better.

'He's got the constitution of an ox. I thought I'd have had to hospitalise him by now,' his doctor told Jane.

'I hope that won't be necessary. He would much rather die here at home.'

'Can you cope with that?' he asked doubtfully.

'He's changed my life. I can cope with anything for him.'

He patted her shoulder. 'You're a good sort. Not many people your age would be bothered with a difficult old man.'

'He isn't difficult with me.'

'Pity you didn't get together sooner. You might have stopped him becoming so crusty with everyone else,' the doctor said drily.

Dick, who had heard about Hector's 'turn' when Jane called off their trip to the coast, had been ringing up every night. As soon as he heard Hector was better, he wanted to fix up a new date, but Jane made excuses.

On Thursday she had a note from Adam, written on a correspondence card enclosed in an envelope—an expensive envelope made of thick cream paper with a dark blue tissue lining. The card had his London address printed along the top of it.

Below this, using dark blue ink and a split nib which gave his strongly formed hand the elegant style lacked by ball-point and fibre-tip writing, he had written:

I thought you might like to see our house and my mother's dolls' house. Is 7 p.m. convenient? Let me, or Dad, know if it isn't. Looking forward to seeing you. Adam.

In the box containing her most treasured possessions, Jane had a paper napkin from a fast-food café where she and Nick had once had a meal together. On the napkin, in Biro, he had written, 'You are the most beautiful girl in the world. I love you'.

She had kept it—and would always keep it—as her first and only love-letter.

As she re-read Adam's card, studying the way he formed his capital letters and signed his name clearly and boldly, not with an illegible squiggle like her former boss, she would have liked to believe that in years to come the card would be stored in her treasure box.

But she had an uneasy feeling that by this time next year it was more likely to represent a foolish and, for her, painful interlude rather than the early stages of a lasting love-affair.

She gave a great deal of thought to what to wear for her visit to the Manor.

There would have been more choice had it been autumn or winter. Most of the clothes in Mrs Chichester's pre-war wardrobe, or at least those which had survived, were more suitable for those seasons than for summer wear.

After much debate, she decided on the dress she had worn at Dick's party.

On Friday morning she drove to the nearest market town to have her hair cut at a salon recommended by Rosamund Farnham as the only place with a first-class stylist.

Before her appointment, Jane bought some sheer tights, a new lipstick and an eyeshadow palette. The lipstick was an extravagance as the colour she wanted was only to be had in one of the expensive brands, but the assistant gave her a sample bottle of a scent which was even more expensive.

Hector assumed she was spending the evening with Dick. She felt badly about not being frank with him, but knew the truth would put him in a towering rage which wouldn't be good for him.

When she went out at night she always left a telephone number where she could be contacted in an emergency. Hector dismissed this precaution as unnecessary fussing and never looked at the number she left on the pad. She could only hope that, if he should glance at it tonight, he wouldn't recognise it as that of his arch enemies. But the risk seemed preferable to leaving him on his own with no way of contacting her if he felt poorly.

'You look very comely, my dear,' he said, when she was ready to leave. 'That old bird you lived with in London had taste as well as money. Must have had a good figure too, when she was young. I don't care for the way women dress now. Look like tarts, most of 'em. Or scarecrows. Or members of a coven. Don't dress to look pretty and ladylike any more. Power-dressing. Pah! Twaddle! Any girl who looks the way you do can twist a man round her little finger.'

Jane laughed. 'I'd like to believe you, Hector. Actually power-dressing is passé. I'm not sure what the latest "in" look is. It's usually gone out by the time I've caught up with it. I did have a skim through *Vogue* at the hairdresser's this morning, but the clothes they show are always wildly expensive and often impractical for ordinary women's lives.'

As she kissed him goodbye, he said, 'You smell nice too. That's not Je Reviens, is it? Always liked that scent.'

'No, this is Paloma, named after Paloma Picasso, daughter of the painter. I was given a tiny sample bottle this morning by a cosmetic salesgirl.'

'That's another thing... you know how to paint your face... don't overdo it like some I've seen. Off you go. Have a good time. If he pops the question, don't say yes, say maybe. Never does any harm to let 'em stew for a bit.'

On the way to the Manor, Jane wondered if Dick would be angry if he could see her now, setting out to have dinner with another man.

Common sense told her he was far more likely to 'pop the question', as Hector put it, than Adam. But even he might think twice if he knew her history. Perhaps, in fairness, to him, she ought to tell him the truth the next time they met.

Was it right to go on seeing him? What would an agony aunt advise in this situation?

By the time she arrived at the Manor's imposing gateway, she had composed the reply she felt an impartial adviser would probably give.

'There is no reason why you shouldn't enjoy a friendly relationship with more than one man, my dear. But if you have reason to believe that one of them is developing deeper feelings towards you, it would be unkind and unfair to encourage him unless his feelings are reciprocated. As for the man whose interest in you is unlikely to be serious, you are risking heartache by continuing to see him. A reputation as a womaniser is rarely without some foundation and such men, although often charming, are best avoided.'

But here I am, like innumerable women before me, ignoring centuries of female experience in the hope that I'll be the exception to the rule, thought Jane as she drove slowly up the straight beech-lined drive to the house which would one day be Adam's.

At its inner end the drive turned so that the house was hidden from the road. It was a tall four-storey house, built about 1700, of bricks which nearly three centuries of wind and weather had turned to a soft rose-red. On either side of the imposing doorway were three tall windows showing the linings of elaborate curtains. Above these was a row of seven slightly shorter windows and above them the windows of attics. There was also a basement floor.

Adam must have been watching for her arrival. As she climbed out of the car and, from force of habit, locked it, he appeared at the top of the steps and ran down them to come and greet her.

'Hello, Jane. You're looking very good.'

As she smiled and said, 'Thank you,' he put both hands on her shoulders and bent to kiss her cheek. 'And you smell delicious. That's Paloma, isn't it?'

'Yes. You must have an excellent nose for scents.'

'Probably because my mother was mad about scented flowers and, when I was small, used to make me close my eyes while she waved something under my nose and I had to guess what it was. She always used to wear a scent called Arpège. Occasionally, walking about London, I catch a whiff of it—usually on a woman of my mother's generation. You weren't wearing Paloma the night we danced at Annabel's . . . or at Ros's supper party.'

The reminder of their embrace by the lake made her glad they were walking towards the house and she could turn her face away, as if looking round the garden, to conceal her heightened colour.

'No, I don't always wear scent.'

'A lot of women wear too much. It should be elusive, not intrusive.' As they reached the foot of the steps, he indicated the barred and shuttered windows of the basement. 'Those used to be kitchens and sculleries but are now storerooms. The whole of the ground floor—which is actually several feet above ground—is furnished in the style of a rather grand private house but everything is for sale. My parents lived on the first floor where the ceilings aren't as high and the rooms are easier to heat. Would you like to look round the "shop" first?'

'Very much.'

As they entered the lofty hall with its graceful staircase curving up to the floors above, Adam said, 'In my mother's time, there were always marvellous flowers everywhere. She had a natural gift for arranging them in imaginative ways. Now someone comes in to do the flowers once a week, but I find her efforts rather contrived. Are you good with flowers?'

'I don't know. I love flowers but I've never had the run of a large garden. In London I had a few pots on a fire escape. Oh . . . what a wonderful room!'

He had opened the door of a large elegant drawing-room. Now she could see that the curtains glimpsed from the drive were made of thick cream silk damask with swagged pelmets trimmed with thick fringes.

It was without question the most beautiful room she had ever entered. The illusion that it was in use was enhanced by the way the furniture was arranged and by touches such as a book left open on the arm of a chair and a basket of embroidery wools and a piece of needlepoint on an end table.

'How lucky you were to grow up with all this, even if the furnishings changed as pieces were sold.'

'Yes—although there are drawbacks. All these windows have to be shuttered and locked and a complex system of alarms activated every night. When my parents first came here, none of those precautions was necessary. There were occasional burglaries then, but they were committed by professionals, without violence or vandalism.'

He looked down at her. 'I hold more than my father's experience against the young thug who broke in here the night we met. If I hadn't had to dash off and leave you...'

He left the sentence unfinished and there was a glint in his eyes which made her turn quickly away, saying, 'Tell me about this table. I've never seen one like it.'

'It's Russian... an architect's table. If you'll hold this jug for a moment—by its base, not the handle—I'll show you how it works.'

Handing her a large creamware jug, he demonstrated the double ratchet system which raised the top of the table to drawing-board height.

The table's country of origin reminded her of his mother's collection of Russian ornaments and also of Hector's allegation that the Fontenays had behaved badly over the Fabergé cat. Perhaps later this evening there would be a chance to find out their side of the story.

'Come and see the dining-room and then we'll go up and have a drink.' Adam slipped his hand under her elbow to steer her across the hall.

He was still dressed for London in a well-cut dark suit with half an inch of shirt cuff and discreet gold cufflinks showing between his sleeve and his hand, and a conservative silk tie.

Yet she knew that inside the conventional tailoring was a body whose power and virility she had felt, briefly, by the lake... and wanted to feel close to her again.

Conscious of her vulnerability, she was glad that in a few minutes' time they would have Colonel Fontenay's presence to keep the situation under control.

The long table in the dining-room was laid as for a formal dinner party with silver candelabra and rare wine glasses reflected in its polished surface. The gold rims and emerald-green borders of a Coalport dinner service gleamed in the late evening sunlight.

Side-tables held other examples of hand-painted porcelain and, while Adam was telling her about them, Jane was aware that most of the time his eyes were on her.

Upstairs on the first-floor landing the appointments were much less grand.

'This is my parents' sitting-room which faces south and west and gets the sun all day,' he said, showing her into a large room decorated in shades of soft peach and full of books and small paintings, many of dogs and other animals.

'What would you like to drink?' he asked, as she looked round, surprised not to see his father there.

Concluding that the colonel must still be changing, Jane said, 'Is white wine possible?'

'It is.' He took a bottle from a modern transparent cooler on the drinks table and filled a glass with a spiral air-twist in its stem.

'Is this glass as rare and valuable as it looks?' she asked, as he gave it to her.

'Possibly, but don't let it worry you. My father believes that good wine tastes better in good glasses, but most of the things we have up here were bought for the proverbial song when he and my mother were starting out in the trade. By the way, he was disappointed that he couldn't join us tonight. He wanted to meet you again but had a long-standing engagement it was impossible to break. So we'll be dining *à deux*.'

As he spoke he was adding soda to brandy and ice. It wasn't until that was done that he looked at her, lifted his glass in an unspoken toast and said, 'You don't mind being alone with me, I hope?'

She did mind, but how could she say so? A long evening alone with Adam sent a tremor of mingled delight and apprehension down her spine.

She remembered, on the night she had met him, Anita's giggly comment when Mrs Chichester had used the same French phrase.

Anita had said, 'I 'ope that don't mean what it sounds like. She could get 'erself into trouble.'

CHAPTER SEVEN

'I WAS looking forward to meeting your father. May I look at all these interesting things?' she asked, with a gesture at the walls and tables crowded with the trophies of a lifetime's collecting.

'By all means. I'll leave you to browse while I go and attend to the supper...courtesy of Fortnum and Mason.'

'Is there anything I can do to help?'

He shook his head. 'It's only a matter of heating things in the oven. I'll be back in a few minutes.'

In his absence, Jane wandered round the room, taking small sips from her glass and pausing beside display tables filled with scent bottles, netsuke, snuff boxes and other covetable objects.

What a happy life the Fontenays must have had, living in a lovely old house, sharing a passion for collecting and watching their son grow up and become a worthy heir to all this. But how sad it had ended prematurely with Mrs Fontenay's illness and early death.

She couldn't help wondering if Adam had known all along that his father would be out tonight. But even if he had, it seemed unlikely that he had seduction in mind when he couldn't be sure what time Colonel Fontenay would return. Most people in that age-group didn't keep late hours even at dinner parties and it might be that the older man's unbreakable engagement wasn't a social event but a meeting of some sort. Probably he was on several local good-works committees.

Somewhat reassured, she continued to browse until Adam reappeared.

Surprised that she hadn't finished her wine, he asked, 'Is it too dry for you?'

'No, it's delicious, but I've been absorbed in looking at everything. You were going to show me your mother's dolls' house.'

'It's in what was her sewing-room at the other end of the corridor.' He refilled his own glass. 'We'll look at it after supper.'

This was doubly reassuring and Jane began to relax.

But then Adam glanced at his watch and said, 'Our meal should be more or less ready. Let's go up, shall we?'

'Up?' she queried.

'To the attics...my part of the house. Before my mother's illness, she often had guests. Over the years, some of the overseas dealers became friends. They were given bedrooms on this floor and I slept in one of the attics, with another as a playroom-cum-den and the rest being used as box-rooms. When I grew up it made sense for me to have my own flat where I could entertain my friends and not disturb my parents if I came home in the small hours. The attics have their own staircase.'

'I see. How convenient,' said Jane.

But this information had reanimated her apprehension. Clearly she couldn't rely on Colonel Fontenay's return putting a brake on Adam's plans for the evening.

As they left what now seemed the safety of his parents' sitting-room for the hazards of his bachelor flat, she wondered how many girls he had entertained on the top floor and how many had spent the night there. Or, if not the whole night, long enough for him to make love to them.

At one end of the corridor he opened a door giving on to a small landing between two narrow flights of stairs.

As he led the way up the ascending flight, she remembered being told by Olivia Chichester that, in her day, a mannerly man always went up and down steep stairs ahead of a female companion, to avoid a close view of her ankles or legs on the way up and to provide a bulwark should she slip on the way down.

Half turning towards her, Adam said, 'In the old days these would have been bare, or laid with something cheap and nasty to muffle the sound of the maids toiling up and down with scuttles of coal and cans of hot water. But even before I had this carpet laid, the staircase was virtually soundproofed by the thickness of our interior walls and doors. The service doors in this house are thicker than most modern front doors. Would you like a quick tour of my quarters before we eat?'

'Yes, very much.'

'My living-room was the maids' dormitory so it's larger than most of the attics. I sleep in the housekeeper's bedroom here, next to the stairs.'

He threw open a door and stood back for her to view a room which was not what she had expected—except that it had a double bed.

But apart from being wide and looking comfortable, even that didn't conform to her idea of the kind of a bed in which an arch-womaniser would notch up another scalp.

'This was the housekeeper's bed,' said Adam, strolling into the room and tapping the curved footrail of the

Victorian iron bedstead. 'I expect she had a feather mattress but I prefer interior springing. Do you like the quilt?'

'Very much,' Jane said sincerely, moving forward to admire the bright patchwork quilt.

'It's American, bought on a visit to Virginia. I started buying paintings of ships when I was about ten . . .' indicating the massed array of sailing ships on the wall behind the bed. 'They were usually quite cheap then.'

Suddenly he moved closer, putting the flat of his hand lightly against the small of her back. 'Let's eat. You can see the rest later.'

As they left his bedroom, she wondered if he had noticed her instinctive stiffening.

Just as his bed had not been what she had expected, the setting for their meal wasn't what she would have visualised for the prelude to a seduction. Instead of soft lights, smoochy music and champagne waiting in an ice bucket, he had set the table in his kitchen. It had the friendly ambience of a French bistro with bentwood chairs, a gingham cloth and a weighted light fitting pulled down to a level which left their faces in shadow but shone brightly over the table.

'My culinary skills are rather limited,' said Adam, as he pulled out a chair for her. 'Most of the things I can cook—steaks, kebabs, bangers, spaghetti—aren't too popular with girls. For the lighter, less fattening stuff, I rely on Marks and Sparks and F and M. We're starting with their country pâté which I think is pretty good.'

They were at the table for an hour and for much of that time Jane relaxed.

When he would have refilled her glass with the red wine chosen for the meal, she said, 'No, thanks. I'd better not as I'm driving.'

The bottle still poised over her glass, Adam said, 'You've had two glasses so far. You can have another without being over the limit by the time you leave.'

'Perhaps, but I'd better play safe.'

He put the bottle back on the table. 'Always, or only as far as your driving licence is concerned?' His expression held a hint of mockery.

'Always,' she answered levelly.

'Wouldn't life be rather dull if everyone always played safe?'

'Perhaps, but most people don't.'

Adam gave her a thoughtful look but didn't pursue the subject.

When they had finished eating a delicious chestnut parfait flavoured with rum and coated with flakes of dark chocolate, he suggested having coffee in the living-room.

'Can't I help you with the dishes?' she asked.

'Apart from our pudding plates, they're already in the machine. I've never lived in the proverbial bachelor's muddle of dirty dishes and mouldy left-overs.'

And when he switched on the main lights and she saw the working area, partially hidden from view from the dining area, it was as clean and orderly as her own kitchen.

'But you have a cleaner, presumably?'

'One of the team of part-timers who deal with the rest of the house comes up here to give my place a weekly once-over. Which reminds me, have you given any more thought to the suggestion I put to you the last time we were together?'

'Yes, I have. If your father had been here, I was going to ask him what he thought about my attempting to follow in Hector's footsteps.'

'How about coming sailing with me on Sunday morning and then having tea here with Dad?'

'I don't know how to sail.'

'You won't have to. I shall be crewing for a friend. You and his girlfriend will only have to look decorative...although later I could borrow a smaller boat and teach you the rudiments if you liked the idea.'

'Perhaps I ought first to find out what sort of sailor I am,' she said. 'But in any case at the moment all my engagements hinge on whether Hector is fit to be left on his own.'

'OK, let's leave it that—if he's all right and the weather is good, I'll pick you up at the post office bus shelter at ten.'

'Fine. I'll look forward to it.'

Somehow these matter-of-fact arrangements for an outing on Sunday made Jane feel she had been mistaken in imagining that after dinner Adam intended to add her to his list of conquests.

The most striking features of his living-room were two brightly painted prancing horses made for a fairground merry-go-round and rescued from a farmer's barn. At the other end of the long room, once lined with housemaids' beds but now comfortably furnished for reading and listening to music, was a collection of curiosities he had bought in his teens.

'They were all classed as junk when I bought them, but now are being taken more seriously—although not by the old school of dealers such as my father,' he said, with a smile. 'And I'm sure you're not very interested in early radio receivers and pre-Great-War telephones. It would be too much to hope that you play billiards, I suppose?'

'I'm afraid not. Why do you ask?'

'Because the best buy I made as a schoolboy was an Edwardian dining-cum-billiard table. It was advertised in the local paper by a young farmer's wife who wanted to refurnish with modern stuff. She was asking eighty pounds for it and I had to sell some of my collection to raise the money. It has an attic to itself. However if you can't play I'm sure we can find something else to do.'

He was standing by a drinks table which also held coffee-making equipment and the sudden turn of his head and the teasing light in his eyes made Jane's heart do a double flip.

She couldn't find anything to say. In fact it was difficult to breathe.

Adam moved a few paces, switched on some unfamiliar music and then turned and came towards her.

'We could dance,' he suggested, still smiling that heart-stopping smile.

The next moment she was in his arms, held lightly but firmly against him, her right hand in his, her left hand automatically coming to rest on his shoulder.

'It's curious how one's impressions of people change. The first time we danced, at Annabel's, you appeared to be far more sophisticated than you seem to me now,' he said, as they started to move in the same slow nightclub shuffle she remembered from that other night.

Jane didn't want to talk about herself. 'Who is this singing?' she asked, as a voice with a foreign accent began a gentle love-song.

'It's a tape from my parents' collection. I didn't have any dance music up here so I borrowed some of their tapes. This is Charles Aznavour singing *Hold Back The Night*. My mother was mad about him. We used to go camping in France and she'd always bring back a tape. My father teased her by calling him Charles Abattoir.'

Was he trying to make her believe she was the first girl who had danced with him up here? Jane wondered.

'I should have expected your parents to prefer classical music,' she murmured.

'They did, but not exclusively. There's a time and place for this kind of music too.' His hold on her tightened slightly. 'Have you ever wanted a night to last forever, Jane?'

She was glad that, her face on a level with his shoulder, she didn't have to meet his eyes.

'Yes, once... a long time ago... when I was much younger.'

'Only once?'

She nodded. 'What about you?'

'More than once, but not for some time. In fact not since that night at Annabel's.'

What did he mean?

In the same moment that she glanced up, Adam released her hand, moving his hand to her face and holding it tilted upwards. Then he bent his head and kissed her.

It wasn't a long kiss. Indeed it was tantalisingly brief. She had scarcely begun to respond before it was over and they were moving again, only this time more closely embraced, with both Adam's arms around her and his cheek against her forehead.

Jane had closed her eyes to be kissed and she kept them closed, unable to resist the magic combination of the Frenchman's caressing tenor and the gentle strength of the Englishman holding her.

As they swayed to the rhythm, their locked bodies slowly revolving, she knew that if they went on like this there could be only one end to it. He was making love to her now, as surely as if she were in his arms on the sofa. This way—just the rhythmic brushing of thigh against thigh—was more subtle but equally seductive. She could feel her resistance weakening with every line of the refrain. Now Adam was humming the melody, a baritone purr which sent sweet shivers down her spine.

Oh, God, did he know what he was doing to her? Had he tried this technique on other girls and found it unfailingly successful?

Prr-prr...prr-prr...

The intrusive sound was the telephone.

'Sorry about this. I forgot to switch on the answerphone.' Adam released her and moved away to turn off the music.

Watching him cross the room to answer the telephone, Jane felt rather heartened. Surely an expert seducer wouldn't have forgotten to divert calls which might come at inconvenient moments?

After a brief conversation which she heard without taking it in, he replaced the receiver and attended to the coffee which by now was ready to drink.

'Cream but no sugar for you?'

'You have a good memory.'

He arched a dark eyebrow. 'You don't remember how I take my coffee?'

'Black?' She made it sound like a query, but it wasn't really a guess. She remembered every detail of their first dinner together.

'Let's sit over here, shall we?' He carried the cups to a low table, stacked with books, in front of a feather-cushioned sofa. 'Would you like a liqueur? There's kirsch, Drambuie and some stuff called Amaretto I won in a charity raffle a few weeks ago. It's made from almonds, I believe.'

'Not for me, thank you.'

'You don't like liqueurs.'

'Not specially. But don't let me stop you.'

'I don't often drink them either. Shall we have some more Aznavour?'

'That would be nice.'

He went to switch on the music, returning to settle himself at the other end of the three-seater sofa, leaving the space of the centre cushion between them.

'You must spend a lot of money on books,' Jane said, looking at the stacks of new hardbacks in shiny covers arranged on the table in front of them.

'I spend a lot of time reading. With sailing, it's my main relaxation. You're too far away. Come closer.'

He intercepted the hand she was stretching towards her coffee and, by lightly circling her wrist, forced her to move towards him. When she shifted, but only to halfway, he moved his own long lean frame so that they were sharing the middle cushion.

'That's better.'

Aware that his left arm was stretched on the cushions behind her and could very easily close round her, Jane took up her cup and saucer.

'Mmm... this is very good coffee.'

'You puzzle me, Jane. When I kiss you, you seem to like it, but most of the time you're not at ease with me, are you? I thought I was reasonably conversant with girls' silent signals, but I'm getting confusing messages. Some seem to say "full steam ahead". Others indicate "back off".'

She put the cup back on the table and sat with her hands in her lap and her eyes on the carousel horses at the end of the room.

'I find your signals equally confusing, Adam. I thought I was coming to dine with you and your father, not in your bachelor quarters. If you'd made that clear, I shouldn't have come tonight. Not because I don't like you or find your company enjoyable, but because...' She paused, searching for words to explain what she meant without sounding priggish.

'Because you don't want to go to bed with me? Is that what you're trying to say?'

'In a nutshell—yes.'

The pause which followed coincided with a pause on the tape. Then Aznavour began to sing in French and Adam asked, 'Never? Or not yet?'

She drew in her breath. To choose either answer would be to lie. A short time ago, when they were dancing, the true answer would have been 'now'. If the telephone hadn't rung...if they had gone on dancing...kissing...if he had scooped her up and carried her here to the sofa or to his bedroom...would she have resisted?

Aloud she said awkwardly, 'Not yet... perhaps not ever. For me, first, there has to be friendship... quite a long friendship.'

He reached past her for his coffee, leaving the saucer on the table so that his left arm was free to encircle her shoulders.

'Good: we both know where we are. So now why don't you relax?' He stretched his long legs under the table, settled himself more comfortably and started to drink his coffee in leisurely sips.

He might know where he was, but Jane still wasn't sure where she was. His agreement—implied but not stated—could be a bluff. He could think all she needed was some more gentle persuasion. And he could be right.

'This is a book which might interest you,' he said, taking his arm away in order to put down his cup and pick up a large volume on Oriental antiquities. 'You never know when something in this field may come into your hands. The box-rooms of country houses, even small ones, yield some extraordinary things.'

He put the book on her lap, but he didn't put his arm round her shoulders again, she noticed, with perverse regret.

Jane opened the book at a page displaying a Chinese dragon robe and a Japan *furisode* of blue silk embroidered with gilt threads.

'Would you like to borrow it?' he asked.

'I'd love to. I'll take great care of it.'

'I only lend my books to people who can be trusted with them. More coffee?'

'Please.'

Watching him going to the drinks table, she wished she had managed a more diplomatic reply to his question than the blunt answer she had given. All men, even the confident ones, were said to have eggshell egos, especially in matters relating to sex.

The trouble was she had so little experience of men. One passionate teenage romance followed by years of nun-like chastity were a poor preparation for handling a man like Adam. Could he have been serious in implying that he hadn't been involved with anyone else since the night he met her?

The Aznavour tape was still playing when they finished their second cups of coffee.

'One more dance and then I'm going to send you home,' Adam said, rising from the sofa and drawing her to her feet.

This time, although the Frenchman was singing a poignant lyric about searching for love, and Adam took her in his arms, he held her loosely, as if they had only just met.

'Tell me,' he said, looking down at her, his eyes quizzical, 'does your definition of friendship preclude kisses?'

She felt the warmth of a blush creeping up her face. 'Not friendly kisses.'

'And where do you draw the line between friendly and other kisses?'

'I'm sure you don't need me to spell that out for you, Adam.'

'Maybe I do. I've never met a girl quite like you.' Suddenly he pulled her close and for a few moments, until the singer's voice faded into silence, she felt the delicious sensation of being heart to heart with him.

He had left the door of his bedroom open. As they passed it on the way to the back staircase, Jane felt a pang of regret for the chance she had turned down and might not be offered a second time.

Would he now write her off as a frigid prude? But surely her response to his kisses must have proved that she wasn't a cold person?

It had not been dark long and, as they left the house, an optical illusion made it seem that the pale summer moon was cruising past a few small stationary clouds.

Adam opened the driver's door for her, leaning inside the car to place the book he was lending her on the front passenger-seat. When he straightened he held the door open, but not wide enough for her to climb in.

Jane said, 'Thank you for a very pleasant evening.'

Adam acknowledged her thanks with an inclination of the head.

'I'm not sure if this will be the right side of your limit, but I'm sure you'll tell me if it isn't.' His free hand came up to her chin, tilting her face to receive a chaste kiss on each of her cheeks. 'How does that suit you?'

She smiled, accepting his mockery with a good-humoured, 'Goodnight, Adam . . . and thank you for the book.'

But when she put her hand on the door to open it wider, he held it still. 'Bring a windcheater with you on Sunday and something to keep your hair out of your eyes. Goodnight.'

He swooped to kiss her again; a long sweet kiss on her mouth. When he stood back, swinging the door open for her, she almost collapsed into the driving seat and although the ignition key was already in her hand her fingers were so unsteady that it took what seemed an eternity of fumbling to fit it into its hole.

In the second before the engine fired, she thought she heard him laugh.

Her nerve-ends were still quivering when she changed down at the gate before turning on to the road.

The following morning, while she was out shopping, Dick telephoned.

'He wants you to look at a house they're going to auction,' Hector told her. 'Wants a woman's opinion of the place. He'll pick you up at two.'

'I had things to do this afternoon. You should have told him I'd ring back.'

'You've nothing to do that won't wait. Do you good to get out in the fresh air. There's a nice teashop in that village. All the cakes are home-made. You can bring me back some of their fudge. I've a weakness for fudge.'

'Why not come with us?' she suggested. She hadn't yet told him she would be out most of Sunday.

Hector shook his head. 'I've seen enough of empty houses. Always hated doing house clearances. I remember when I was a greenhorn, several times I made lump sum offers and by the time I went round to clear the place anything of interest had been taken by the deceased's relations. I was left with the job of dumping a load of smelly bedding and other old rubbish. If you ever do a house clearance, make an inventory beforehand and don't pay until the job's done.'

'He's right, I'm afraid,' Dick agreed, when she reported this advice to him while they were driving to the house he had to look over. 'Supposedly honest people can be amazingly unscrupulous and very few house clearances are worth the effort involved.' He glanced sideways at her. 'Are you still bent on keeping the ol man's shop going?'

'I'm not sure.'

Jane was feeling the effects of a sleepless night. It ha been just after eleven when she had gone to bed, an she had heard the village clock strike midnight and a the small hours.

This morning, roused by her alarm clock, she ha woken up to the knowledge that she was deeply an probably hopelessly in love with a man who, even if hi present intentions were serious, might—probabl would!—change his mind when it came to the crunch

'You sound a bit depressed,' said Dick.

'Not really...just tired. I didn't sleep very well.' T deflect him from asking why, she said, 'Did you rea the piece in this morning's paper about the discovery o another of Turner's sketchbooks at a car-boot sale?'

He had missed the story and wanted to know all th details. He remembered another of the great painter' sketchbooks being discovered in the mid-Eighties an causing enormous excitement in the London art world

Discussing the new discovery and talking about othe treasures which had turned up in unlikely places kep the conversation going for the rest of the journey.

'They say there may be an unrecognised Vermee somewhere in this part of the country because of Eas Anglia's trade links with Holland in the seventeent century,' said Dick, as he parked the car outside the gat of the house they had come to see. 'But none of th paintings we've auctioned has turned out to be a los masterpiece.'

The house was Edwardian, built in 1906 with goo materials and painstaking craftsmanship for a larg family to live in middle-class comfort with all the mod cons of the period. After they had looked round it, Dick revealed that in fact it wasn't his first visit.

'There's a chance it may never come under the hammer,' he told her. 'There's something about this place that appeals to me. I'd like to buy it myself, by private treaty. I want a place of my own again... but most of all I want you. Will you share this house with me, Jane? Will you marry me?'

In spite of Hector's conviction that Dick was courting her, the proposal took her by surprise. Judging by his expression, Dick was somewhat surprised himself. She had the impression that he hadn't meant to commit himself yet but had blurted it out on impulse.

Her reply was equally impromptu. 'Oh, Dick, I can't... it's impossible.'

'Impossible? Why? I thought you liked me.'

'I do... I do. You're a dear, but...' She floundered for a moment, then drew a deep breath before saying, 'Do you realise how little you know about me?'

'I know all I need to know. You're kind... loyal... honest... gentle.'

'I try to be kind. I can't claim to be honest. My whole life—for the past nine years—has been based on deception.'

'That I can't believe,' he said, smiling. 'What are you talking about?'

CHAPTER EIGHT

'I—I'M sorry to give you this shock, Dick. You see, I... well, the truth is I've had a child... a daughter. I'm an unmarried mother.'

As she had known he would, Dick looked dumbfounded. What his deeper reaction might be, she couldn't tell. His expression showed only amazement.

After some seconds, a look of concern replaced the astonishment. 'My poor girl, what happened? Did you lose the baby?'

'Oh, no, she's alive and well. She was taken in by my sister. Her name is Apple. She's coming to stay with me soon. She doesn't know I'm her mother. She thinks I'm her aunt and her godmother.'

At this he frowned, saying, 'I think that's a mistake. It's always best to tell children the truth about these things. They're sure to find out eventually and then it upsets them far more than if they grow up knowing the truth. What made you take that decision? Was it your sister's idea?'

'It wasn't a decision as such. It just... came about. I agree it's not a good thing. I can only explain it by telling you the whole story. But you may not want to hear it... now that you know truth about me.'

'Don't be silly. Of course I want to hear it. The fact that you've had a baby doesn't alter my feelings towards you. Why should it? You haven't revealed something shameful... only a very common, sad, forgivable dilemma that thousands of nice girls have found themselves in. I take it your daughter's father was the boy you told me about... the one who was killed avoiding someone else's baby?'

Jane nodded. 'If it hadn't been for the accident, we would have married...even though we were far too young and had no money. It wasn't a casual affair. We really did love each other. But my father wouldn't believe that. He thought I was bad...promiscuous. He threw me out. If it hadn't been for Alice and Bill, I don't know what I'd have done.'

'He actually threw you out?' Dick looked more shocked by this than by her first revelation. 'But that's a Victorian attitude.'

'Both my parents were teachers...missionary teachers. They weren't as narrow-minded as my grandparents. According to my aunt—my father's sister—her parents were incredibly rigid in their attitudes. She had no freedom at all until she married. After my mother died in an epidemic in Nigeria, my father became more and more like his father. When he came back to England to live with my aunt and me—she was a widow by then—he became a domestic tyrant. If it hadn't been for Aunt Dee, I should never have been allowed out. She and I conspired against him, which was wrong, I know, but a man as austere as Father forces people to disobey him. He never laughed. He had absolutely no sense of humour.'

'Well, you certainly have,' said Dick. 'You must have got it from somewhere.'

'Perhaps from Aunt Dee. She was a great one for jokes... a lovely person.'

'How did she react when you told her about the baby?'

'She never knew about it. I was plucking up my courage to tell her when she was taken ill and died. It was all very sudden. That left just Father and me. Whether he'd have thrown me out if I hadn't had Alice to turn to, I'm not sure. Perhaps not. And of course there are hostels where girls without supportive parents can stay till their babies are born. It isn't like long ago when, if their families disowned them, girls threw themselves in the river. There are all kinds of social services to advise and help unmarried mums.'

'Even so it must have been a rotten situation for you on top of losing the boy you were in love with. I can imagine what you went through.' Dick reached for her hand and covered it with his.

As she talked Jane had been absently playing with the strap of her shoulder bag. Now her fingers stilled and she looked up and met his eyes. Seeing only kindness and sympathy in them, she felt the prickle of tears behind her own eyes.

Probably he was one of the few men who did have some insight into the loneliness and misery of the first months of her pregnancy. Would Adam understand? She doubted it. He would most likely think her a fool for being too naïve to avoid her predicament.

And of course she had been a fool... reckless, impulsive, irresponsible. She could not deny those charges. But she had paid for her foolishness; paid a thousand times over, first with her grief for Nick and later for Apple, her baby. Even now, all these years later, it still caused her a pang to remember the day she had given her daughter into the care of her sister.

Dick saw she was close to tears. 'What you need is a nice cup of tea. There's a pleasant place here in the village. Come on; we can talk it out there.'

Like most country teashops, the Blue Barn did better business when the weather was wet. At half-past three on a warm afternoon, they had the place to themselves apart from a middle-aged couple and a frail man in a wheelchair who looked as if he might be a resident at a nearby old people's home being taken out for tea by his son and daughter-in-law.

'Let's sit outside, shall we?' said Dick, steering her through the main tearoom to a small garden at the back where several tables were set out.

When a girl came to take their order, without consulting Jane he asked for a selection of sandwiches, some of the café's date and walnut cake and a pot of Darjeeling tea.

'They do very good sandwiches here. All their bread is home-made and the fillings are a cut above the usual stale cheese and mushy tomato. You don't dislike dates, I hope. We could have something else, if you'd rather?'

Jane smiled and shook her head. Although by now she had recovered herself, she had no idea how to handle his proposal of marriage. Her main feeling was one of relief that he now knew the truth about her.

'It will be more crowded later,' said Dick. 'But I've heard that what keeps the place going are the take-away cheesecakes and other fancy puddings the proprietress makes to order. Someone was telling me that a lot of the sweet things served at dinner parties in this part of the county come from here.'

'Hector thought we might come here. He asked for some of their fudge. Don't let me forget it when we go.'

'I'll take some for Tommy,' said Dick. 'He would have liked to come with me this afternoon but I wanted to have you to myself.'

At this point the waitress returned with their pot of tea. 'Your sandwiches won't be long. They're all freshly made. Are you on holiday?' she asked.

Business being slack, she stayed talking to them until a woman with grey hair put her head out of a window and said, 'The sandwiches are ready, Hazel.'

The sandwiches were as delicious as Dick had promised and Jane made a show of enjoying them although she was not really hungry.

'You were going to tell me how it happened that your little girl doesn't know you're her mother,' Dick reminded her gently.

'I'm only her biological mother,' she said sadly. 'Alice is her real mother. She's brought her up...given her love and care...nursed her, taught her, provided for her. All I did was give birth to her and contribute what money I could, which was never very much.'

'Does your sister have other children?'

'Yes. Three boys. Alice is older than I am. Six years older. It was always her ambition to marry and have a large family. But when both the twins were boys, she hoped her next child would be a girl. When it turned out to be a third boy and the doctor advised her against trying again, she was very disappointed. Then, much to her delight, my baby was a girl, which Alice said was the next best thing to having a daughter herself. Bill was pleased, too. He's a very good husband and father...perhaps too indulgent in some ways. I hoped he would take my side in the argument over telling Apple the truth. But he always takes Alice's part, even if he doesn't really agree with it.'

'Why was your sister against the child knowing the truth?'

'She wasn't—not at first. When we discussed it, at the very beginning, it was agreed that she would be told I was her mother as soon as she could take it in. But then later on, when I thought Apple was old enough to have it explained to her in simple terms, Alice didn't agree. She said it was the wrong moment. It's always been the wrong moment. And I can't tell Apple if my sister won't. How can I?'

'An awkward situation,' he agreed. 'And the longer it's put off, the more difficult it will become. Surely your sister must see that?'

'She loves Apple. She doesn't want to lose her. And I think she feels that when Apple finds out she may want to live with me. In London I couldn't have had her. There was no room and I was at work all day. But here it's different. I could look after her.'

'And you want her? That's the main thing. You would like to have her living with you?'

'I've always wanted her, Dick. I should never have let her go if it had been possible to keep her. But I had a struggle to keep my own head above water. It was the best thing for her to let Alice have her. But now I don't think she's happy. The three boys are so boisterous and noisy and she's a quiet, dreamy child. She doesn't really fit into that family.'

He was silent, his hand still on hers. 'Your situation is still rather insecure. Perhaps that worries your sister. If you were married...had someone to care for you...she might feel differently.'

Jane withdrew her hand from his light clasp. 'She might...but what is more certain is your mother's reaction. She doesn't like me, Dick. She'll like me even less when you tell her.'

'Whatever gives you that idea?'

'It's not an idea. It's a fact. I knew it the first time we met. Women sense these things. Our intuition is more developed than yours. We pick up signs which men miss. Perhaps there's someone else she thinks would make you a good wife. Someone local. I'm an outsider.'

'Who I marry is up to me...nothing to do with my mother.'

But his answer was a tacit admission that Jane's instinct was correct; Mrs Osborne *was* dubious about her and had made that clear to her son.

She said, 'But your mother's instinct may be right. Sometimes wise, loving parents do know what's best for their children, even grown-up children. Your mother strikes me as a sensible woman. What was her attitude to your wife?'

'They were very fond of each other...got on like a house on fire.'

'There you are, then. She isn't being possessive or difficult. Her attitude to me is based on much sounder feelings. She knows how lonely you are. She doesn't want to see you rush into a second marriage which, later, you may regret.'

'Jane, is this a roundabout way of turning me down? Are you trying to tell me that you quite like my company but that's as far as it goes?' He paused before adding, 'That you couldn't face going to bed with me?'

She felt herself starting to flush. 'I—I've never thought about it.'

'Well, try thinking about it, will you? Try imagining the four of us living together in the house I showed you...you and me and Tommy and Apple. Why did you call her Apple?'

'If she'd been a boy I was going to call her Nick...Nicholas. I couldn't decide on a girl's name. There were no family names I liked. Right up to the time she was born, I still hadn't picked out a name for a daughter. And then, a few hours before I went into hospital, Alice brought home some apples and I suddenly thought, that's it—Apple. Almost everybody likes apples and girls have been named after flowers, months and jewels. I was at school with a girl whose nickname was Peach. So why not Apple? Do you think it's a silly name?'

'Not at all...and I'm looking forward to meeting her. When is she coming?'

'Some time during the school holidays...depending on Hector's health. I used to spend my holidays with my sister and her husband, but this will be the first time I've had Apple to stay with me.'

Dick said, 'Sally and I were hoping to have two children, a boy and a girl. If things pan out as I hope, I'll be the father of three...my boy...your girl...and one we've made between us. It would be good for you, Jane...to have another baby that you knew would be welcome and could love and care for yourself. It would make up for all you've gone through.'

'Oh, Dick, you're so kind, but...'

'But what?' he prompted, when she left her reply unfinished. 'If it's only my mother's attitude which is worrying you, forget it. I'm old enough to make my own decisions.'

He shifted his chair closer to hers and laid his arm along the back of it.

'Is there something else on your mind?'

There was a great deal on her mind, chiefly that she was in love with someone else. But she shrank from telling Dick that.

'Listen,' he said, 'you don't have to make up your mind now. There's no hurry. Take your time. Think it over. I know it's not a decision to be taken lightly. We're neither of us young and impetuous. We've both been through some tough times.'

As she searched for a suitable answer which would neither hurt him nor give him false expectations, his arm moved from the back of her chair to around her shoulders.

'We have so much in common, my dear. The shared experience of a painful bereavement. We each have a child we love. We both like a quiet country life.'

Apart from the mention of children, he sounded, she thought, like an elderly man proposing a marriage of companionship to an elderly woman. But they were not even middle-aged. They were still young, with the best of their lives still ahead of them. Dick himself, under the influence of several drinks, had said an ardent good-night to her after the party.

She said, choosing her words carefully, 'I think perhaps you *are* being impetuous, Dick. You'd like a place of your own again and now there's a house which appeals to you... and a woman who's on her own—or will be when Hector dies—and who brings out your protective instinct. But do we really have what it takes to make a marriage work? We both need someone, that's for sure. But do we need each other? Am I really the right person for you?'

'I think so... in fact I know it.' Taking her by surprise, for she wouldn't have thought he would ever do it in public, he turned her face to his and kissed her lightly on the lips. 'It isn't only someone to keep house for me and be a mother to Tommy that I need, Jane. I want to be able to hold you in my arms... to have you beside me at night when I can't sleep... when I need you.'

Clearly it was difficult for him to express his deepest feelings in words, and she shared his embarrassment. Not only because this was not the right place to discuss such personal emotions but because she wasn't ready to hear these things from him and didn't think she ever would be.

Yet at the back of her mind a small voice was saying, Wait. Don't turn him down flat. This is a good, kind man. They don't grow on trees. Do as he says. Think it over. Don't reach for the moon and find yourself left with a handful of stardust.

Waiting for Adam to pick her up from the bus shelter the following morning, Jane remembered the manner of their parting and wondered if, although they would be spending the day with other people, somehow he would find or make an opportunity to repeat that final kiss.

He might even kiss her hello. The thought of it sent a quiver through her.

If only it were Dick who made her feel like this, she thought, with a sigh. Perhaps, if she had never met Adam, she might have found Dick more attractive. It might be that physical attraction was largely a visual reaction. Maybe, if she were to be blindfolded or shut in a dark place, where both Adam and Dick came in without speaking and kissed her, she wouldn't be able to tell the difference. It might be that, given the opportunity, Dick would be a wonderful lover who could thrill her to the marrow of her being.

Anyway there was far more to marriage than sleeping together. After the honeymoon period, sex played a relatively small part in the relationship. An important part. A lovely part. But not the whole part or even fifty per cent of it.

She wanted Adam now, desperately. But would she hunger for his touch if they had been living together for years?

But if it isn't a burning need at the beginning, how can it last a lifetime? argued another part of her mind.

She was still debating with herself when she saw Adam's car approaching.

Probably, if she had waited, he would have got out to open the nearside door for her. But she opened it for herself and got in quickly, smiling and saying, 'Good morning,' with what she hoped was an air of total self-possession.

'Good morning.'

Was it her imagination or was Adam's greeting slightly brusque?

'I hope I'm suitably dressed,' she said, as he checked his rear-view mirror before putting the car back in gear.

He glanced briefly at her jeans and shirt. 'You look fine to me.'

'I've got shorts and a sweatshirt in my tote-bag, in case it gets hotter or cooler.'

'Good. I was listening to some Mozart. Do you mind if I finish it?'

'Of course not.'

Now she was almost certain that something had annoyed him. Or maybe he was always uptight in the early part of the day.

This theory seemed to be proved when, after driving the whole way without speaking, his manner reverted to normal at the rendezvous with his friends.

She liked them both on sight. Jack was a big, weatherbeaten man in his forties and Louisa looked about Adam's age. They had different surnames but appeared to be partners. Jane wondered why they weren't married. Maybe they had been married, to other people, and it hadn't worked out.

Jack's boat was called *Harnser*. When she asked what it meant, he said was an East Anglian folk name for a heron.

During the morning it struck Jane that, although Adam seemed to have cheered up and even made several jokes, most of his conversation was directed at Jack and Louisa. He wasn't saying much to her. In fact hardly anything.

It was true that he was the crew and that kept him fairly busy because *Harnser* was quite a big boat with a tiny galley, a saloon, and a cabin with a rather oddly shaped double bunk.

'She sleeps four... two on the banquettes,' Louisa explained, showing Jane round. 'Adam has been across the North Sea with us several times.'

As a threesome or a foursome? Jane wondered.

She and Louisa spent most of the morning sitting on cushions on the deck, chatting about this and that. Every so often Louisa would go below to make some more coffee and then Jane would have a chance to watch the two men.

Adam was wearing shorts and a French-looking T-shirt with navy and sand-coloured stripes. His long legs were brown and not as hairy as Jack's legs. From time to time he came past and stepped over the women's outstretched legs, but when Louisa was below he didn't seize the opportunity to give Jane an intimate smile or a discreet caress. She was forced to the conclusion that he was deliberately ignoring her.

But why? What could she have done to annoy him? She hadn't seen him since the night before last and he hadn't been annoyed with her then.

Could it be that, thinking it over, he had become peeved by the limits she had set on their relationship? If a man was accustomed to girls who jumped into bed without thinking twice about it, no doubt he would find it rather tiresome to be denied that pleasure. But surely nowadays, with AIDS added to the other hazards of promiscuity, weren't most people being more cautious?

After three hours out on the sea, they returned to *Harnser*'s moorings, there to share a picnic lunch and a bottle of wine.

By this time Jane had discovered that Jack was an orthopaedic surgeon at a London teaching hospital and Louisa taught art a nearby girls' boarding-school. Jack's daughter was one of her pupils.

When, in answer to their questions, Jane had revealed some of her background, Jack said, 'I wish I could emulate you, Jane, and move to the country permanently.' He turned to Adam. 'You could, you lucky devil. I can't think why you don't.'

Adam shrugged. 'I contemplate it from time to time.' He glanced at his watch. 'We had better be moving. Thanks for the lunch, Louisa.'

'And thank you for including me,' said Jane, as he rose to go. 'I've enjoyed it enormously.'

'Good. You must come again. Next time we'll put you to work... teach you a spot of seamanship,' Jack said jovially.

Smiling, Jane said she would look forward to it—while privately doubting that there would be a next time. There was now no doubt in her mind that Adam was furious with her. The reason was still a mystery, but every instinct told her it was so.

As they began the drive back he didn't switch on the tape-player or the radio, but nor did he speak.

Jane had no intention of spending the journey in silence. She said briskly, 'You invited me to tea with your father, but I don't think I'll come if you don't mind.'

She sensed rather than saw that this statement surprised him.

'Oh... why is that?' he enquired.

'Because, although I'd like to meet your father, it's fairly obvious you're not in a sociable mood—or not as far as I'm concerned—and I've had enough of being cold-shouldered.'

He didn't deny that he had been cold towards her. For a few moments it seemed he was going to ignore her statement. Then, just as Jane's indignation had reached boiling point and she was about to tell him that she couldn't stand people who sulked, he turned the car into a lay-by, braked and switched off the engine.

Turning to face her, he said, 'Last night I went to a dinner party given by an architect whose wife is a solicitor. She doesn't have much time to spare so her rul for entertaining is to have a cold course, a cooked cours and a bought course. Last night's bought course was truffle torte from the Blue Barn. When she went to collec it yesterday afternoon, she saw you and Dick Osborn in the garden. You don't know her but she know you...has been to your shop. Most people hereabout know Dick and she thought it would be of general interes to tell us that he seemed to have found a replacemen for his late wife. She had drawn that conclusion fron the fact that he had his arm round you.'

After a pause, he added icily, 'I forbore to point ou that rather less than twenty-four hours earlier I had ha the same privilege.'

CHAPTER NINE

STUNG by his sarcasm, Jane said, 'Well, that was chivalrous of you, Adam. But it might have been better to point out that an arm round somebody's shoulders isn't conclusive evidence of a serious relationship.'

'Perhaps not, but I don't think Dick Osborne is the type to kiss a girl in public unless he is serious,' he snapped back. 'Are you playing with him, Jane?'

'No, I am not!' she said indignantly.

'Then I'm forced to conclude you're playing with me—as you did before,' he said curtly. 'I'll take it once, but not twice. Dick may not have a short fuse, but I do. Light mine and you're liable to get burnt.'

The next instant she was in his arms and he was kissing her in a manner totally different from Friday night's civilised kisses.

Although she had made love before, if not very often, Jane had never experienced a kiss anything like this. It wasn't the savage assault on her lips she had expected from her glimpse of the angry glitter in his eyes before he swooped on her. That she could have resisted and survived.

Instead he chose to punish her by leaping all the intermediate states in between attraction and consummation and kissing her as if they were already lovers, not in a car parked in a lay-by but alone in a dark private place where it wouldn't be long before he possessed her completely.

The effect on Jane, when at last he let her go, was almost as if he *had* possessed her. For several minutes afterwards she felt totally disorientated, every nerve, every tissue, every cell of her being thrown into wild confusion by sensations she had read about, and dreamed about, but never actually experienced.

Aghast, almost disbelieving, she realised that with one consummately sensuous kiss Adam had brought her to a pitch far beyond anything she had experienced in Nick's arms. For a few traumatic seconds all her nerve-ends had quivered with a pleasure of such intensity that she had wanted to cry out, and perhaps would have done so, had her lips not been sealed by his.

By the time she was capable of rational thought, the car was in motion again.

How could he drive? she wondered incredulously. Surely it must have had some effect on him too?

A covert glance at his hands, one resting lightly on the gear lever, the other holding the wheel, showed that both were as steady as a surgeon's.

She was afraid to look at his face for fear he might look at her and guess what the kiss had done to her. She couldn't bear him to know. Somehow, between wherever they were at the moment and where he dropped her off she had to recover herself enough to part company from him with at least a semblance of dignity.

That he had no intention of dropping her off didn't dawn on her until, suddenly, the gates of the Manor came in view. As he stopped the car in the roadway to wait for an oncoming car to pass, she said, 'You must be out of your mind! I'm not having tea here now.'

'Why not? My father's expecting you.'

Adam swung the car across the road and between the tall brick piers supporting two old stone urns.

'My God! You've got gall,' she exploded. 'All day you virtually ignored me. Then you . . . you damn nearly rape me. And now you have the nerve to expect me to come and be polite to your father.'

He glanced at her then, a look which fuelled her wrath by having a definite gleam of amusement in it.

'I plead guilty to the first charge. The second is a nonsense and you know it. I kissed you. Not, I agree, a chaste kiss on your virginal cheek. But we have kissed before, you may recall, and you didn't appear to dislike it.'

She turned her face to the window. 'I've disliked your behaviour today.'

By now they had reached the sweep in front of the house. Adam stopped the car and switched off before he said, 'Would you like me to apologise?'

Before she had formed her answer, he went on, 'I wonder how you would have felt if you'd gone somewhere last night and heard that I had been seen canoodling with a girl in a café?'

'Your hostess was exaggerating. Dick and I weren't canoodling.'

'Are you saying he didn't kiss you?'

'No . . . but it wasn't the way you make it sound. If you must know——'

She stopped short. If she told him Dick had proposed to her it might make matters worse. In any case a proposal was confidential. She had no right to reveal it.

'It wasn't the way your hostess may have described it,' she finished. 'And it doesn't excuse your being hateful to me today.'

'Hateful?' Suddenly his palm was cradling her cheek, turning her face towards him. 'Did you really hate it? I didn't. I'd like to do it again.' As he said this, his thumb traced the outline of her mouth in a caress as gentle as a butterfly kiss. 'But I won't... not now.'

His fingers slid down her cheek and, with a light pinch on her chin, the kind of playful gesture a grown-up might make to a child who had been upset, he turned away and swung his long frame out of the car.

She watched him walk round the front to open the passenger door for her and wondered if he was capable of forcing her into the house.

She wasn't sure how to interpret the fact that it had been jealousy which had made him offhand with her all day. And there wasn't time to think it through now. Nor, still shaken by that kiss, was she in the mood to clash wills with him.

'All right, I'll come in for a short time.' She stretched for the strap of her tote-bag which was on the back seat but out of reach.

'I'll get it.' Adam let go of her door to open the one behind it and reach into the back.

As he did so she slid quickly out, moving away from the car to put a long arm's length between them. If he noticed and recognised the evasive manoeuvre, he didn't show it.

After a glance at his watch, he said, 'We've timed it well. Dad likes his tea sharp at four. It's a quarter to. Would you like to wash your hands?'

'Yes, please.'

He showed her the downstairs cloakroom and handed over the tote-bag. 'We'll be upstairs in the drawing-room. Do you remember the way?'

'Yes, thank you.'

With relief, she closed the heavy mahogany door and leaned against it for a moment, wondering how to get through an hour of making polite conversation to his father when her thoughts and emotions were still in turmoil.

Was Adam's anger about her being seen with Dick an indication that he was beginning to care about her? Or did it mean only that he resented her spending time with anyone else while he was interested in her? Although possibly only until he had lost interest.

Putting the conundrum aside to grapple with later, she went into the inner washroom and spent a few minutes combing her hair and putting on lipstick. Luckily she hadn't been wearing any when Adam had unsnapped her seatbelt and grabbed her or it would have been smeared all over the place.

Remembering his kiss, she felt an involuntary spasm of pleasure streak through her, like the aftershock from an earthquake. If he could do that to her with a kiss, what would it like if she gave him *carte blanche*? Maybe that was what she should do; get him out of her system and then settle down to a life of peace and contentment with Dick. But, having once tasted ecstasy, could one ever be content with less?

'My dear Miss Taunton, how very nice to see you again,' said Colonel Fontenay, coming forward to greet her when she entered the drawing-room, the door having been left open for her.

On her way up the staircase, Jane had resolved to carry off having tea with him with all the aplomb she could muster.

As they shook hands, she smiled and said, 'Won't you call me Jane? I've brought you a cake. It may be coals to Newcastle, but I bought it at the Blue Barn yesterday, after trying a slice while having tea with a friend. It was so delicious I thought you might like one. But perhaps you've had it before. It's the Blue Barn's date and walnut cake.'

'How extremely kind of you, Jane. Did Adam tell you I had a weakness for cake? Come and sit down. Have you had an enjoyable day? The weather was right for it.'

'Yes, perfect. I enjoyed the sailing very much. It was a new experience for me, and Adam's friends are delightful.'

'I think so too. They've dined here on several occasions. It's a bit of a mystery to me why Louisa is still unmarried. In my day she would have been snapped up long since. But perhaps she prefers her independence. No doubt she gets a good salary. Ah, here comes our tea.'

A middle-aged woman in a pinafore had come in with a tray. She said, 'Good afternoon, miss,' to Jane, and then busied herself with spreading an old-fashioned starched cloth with a crocheted border over a gate-leg table before arranging the tea things.

'Not many people seem to have afternoon tea nowadays, but I like it,' said the colonel. 'Crumpets and muffins in the winter, or hot buttered scones. Bread and butter and jam with cake at this time of year. What sort of jam have we today, Mrs Button?'

'Raspberry and greengage today, sir.'

'Miss Taunton has brought me a cake so we'll need another plate.'

Adam said, 'I'll fetch it, Mrs B. Save your legs.'

Jane saw him and the home help exchange smiles. Perhaps she had known him since he was a schoolboy and she a young wife, part-timing to help make ends meet.

After Mrs Button had gone and while Adam was still downstairs, his father said, 'How is Hector Beccles these days? Not too good, I understand?'

'No, I'm afraid not. I think he's only hanging on by will-power,' she said sadly. 'I don't really like leaving him, but he insists I do. He's a very independent man and can't stand being fussed over.'

'He's lucky to have you looking after him.'

'Actually I'm the lucky one. I'm much happier living with Hector than I was working in London. Colonel Fontenay, do you think it would be madness for me to attempt to carry on the business after Hector dies as, sadly, he will before long?'

'Well, he hasn't had a bad run. None of us goes on forever. As to your question . . . I can't advise you, my dear. My view is biased by the fact that I need an assistant here and, from all my son tells me, you would fill the post admirably.'

'Adam may over-estimate my capabilities.'

He shot a keen look at her. 'I doubt that. My son is a good judge of character. I respect his opinions. We have tea at the table, nursery-fashion. Will you sit here?' He drew out a chair for her.

Having seated himself, he went on to outline the changes he had seen in the trade since he and his wife started up.

Jane tried to listen attentively but her concentration was still shot to pieces by what had happened in the car and it didn't help when Adam re-entered the room.

'I've suggested to Jane that, when Hector Beccles dies, it might be easier for her to come here as my assistant than attempt to "go it alone" as the saying goes,' said his father.

'What was her reaction?' asked Adam, looking at her.

'As long as Hector is alive, I'm totally committed to him,' said Jane. She turned to the older man. 'But I do appreciate your offer and I'll think it over. The chance to work in this beautiful house is very tempting. On the other hand I feel it's a challenge to try to keep Hector's business going. Once before in my life I was faced with a challenge and I took what could be called the soft option. I've regretted it ever since. With hindsight, playing safe wasn't the right thing to do. Perhaps it never is. You and your wife weren't playing safe when you started your business, Colonel Fontenay.'

'Very true, but being greenhorns we had no idea what a hazardous enterprise we were undertaking,' he replied, with a rueful smile. 'The antiques trade was always a risky way to make a living, and the risks are far greater now than when Laura and I opened up here.'

'I've heard your wife collected things made by Fabergé. I'd love to see her collection. But perhaps you keep it in the bank now?'

'No, no...it's still here. We have made it more secure, but my wife wouldn't like to think of her treasures being packed away in a strong box. After tea I'll show them to you.'

The late Mrs Fontenay's collection of Fabergé was housed behind glass, on glass shelves, in an alcove in the small room known as the sewing-room.

'My wife made most of her clothes, and she also became very skilled at repairing old textiles,' the colonel explained, while Adam was disconnecting the special alarm system protecting the Fabergé objects. 'Most of the curtains in this house were bought at country-house sales and mended and altered by Laura long before the present vogue for antique curtains, old silk tassels and so on.'

He showed Jane the standing embroidery frame, itself an antique, on which Laura Fontenay had painstakingly repaired pieces of Berlin woolwork and other forms of old needlework which had been damaged by moths. A Victorian beaded teacosy, some of its beads missing, was spread on her work-table, waiting to be renovated. Hundreds of coloured glass beads, spangles, and spools and cards of thread were stored in the many small drawers of a cabinet beside the table.

By this time Adam had the Fabergé alcove open and ready for inspection.

'When the Queen had her Silver Jubilee in 1977,' said Colonel Fontenay, 'as a compliment to her the Victoria and Albert Museum put on a splendid exhibition of Fabergé. A lot of the exhibits came from the royal collection at Sandringham, others from private collections all over the world. My wife lent a couple of her things. One was this delightful snail which had been a courtship present from Adam's maternal great-grandfather to his prospective bride.'

He took the snail from its place and gave it to Jane to hold on the palm of her hand.

'The body of the snail is chalcedony and the shell is translucent jasper,' said Adam.

A few moments ago he had moved away from the alcove and finding him close behind her made Jane give a slight start.

She said, 'I'm not very keen on live snails, but this is beautiful. The shell has such lovely colours in it . . . blue-grey, brown, mauve, pale green . . .'

'Yes, it's a nice piece,' said the colonel, removing it from her hand and replacing it with an almost ball-shaped red elephant. 'This was the other piece Laura lent to the V and A.'

'What is the red stone it's carved from?' she asked.

'Purpurine. Interesting stuff. The secret of how to make it was discovered by someone working at the imperial glass factory in St Petersburg. A similar substance had been made in the eighteenth century by lapidaries at the famous Venetian glassworks at Murano.'

Adam said, 'My mother found Jumbo, as she called him, in a box of assorted junk at a bring and buy sale. At first glance she took him for a ball of sealing wax. For a long time we didn't know he was Fabergé.'

'This rather depressed looking hippo was a present from Adam on our twenty-fifth wedding anniversary,' his father added.

The collection, begun with an heirloom and formed in the thirty years Mrs Fontenay had been a partner in the business, didn't consist exclusively of animals. It included two parasol handles, several photograph frames and a linked pair of clasps for holding a cloak together. But obviously it was the miniature animals which had appealed most strongly to Adam's mother. There were monkeys and mice, several pigs, two owls and more than one cat. Which was the one Adam had bought at Hector's shop? Jane wondered.

Was the fact that neither man mentioned this an indication that there had been something shady about the purchase, something they preferred to ignore?

As, at her host's invitation, she examined the exquisite workmanship of the pieces, she couldn't help feeling it was decidedly odd not to mention that one of the cats had come from Hector.

'In England, it was Queen Alexandra who started the vogue for these little toys and ornaments in the late Victorian, early Edwardian period,' said the colonel. 'As you know, she was a Danish princess before she married Edward VII, and her sister was married to Tsar Alexander III, the penultimate Tsar of Russia. Alexandra would have seen pieces like these on her visits to Russia. Later on, the King commissioned much more elaborate ornaments as birthday presents for her.'

'Are the pieces marked?' Jane asked.

'Some of them, yes. But——' At that moment the telephone rang and the older man said, 'Excuse me, will you? Adam will show you the marks.'

He left the room to take the call somewhere else.

Adam picked up a magnifying glass lying on one of the shelves and handed it to Jane. Then he selected an engraved cigarette case and showed her the mark which, magnified, was revealed as the head of a woman, in profile, and wearing what looked like a large tiara.

'That Russian gold mark is called a *kokoshnik* from the name of the traditional head-dress,' he explained. 'Before 1896, St Petersburg had its own cypher and so did Moscow. We know the case was made in St

Petersburg because it has the name Fabergé, in Russian characters, followed by the workmaster's initials.'

'How are the little animals marked?' she asked.

'They aren't. If you find a hardstone or semi-precious gemstone carving with Russian characters on it, it won't be a Fabergé piece. Respect for the beauty of the material was always his first consideration. Carvings from his workshops were never signed, even on the underside.'

'So there's no way of knowing for certain that all these animals are Fabergé?'

'Only by the excellence of the design and the carving. Fabergé had extremely exacting standards. Not all the pieces made in the workshops passed muster. Only the best were good enough to be sold. He's quoted as saying, "Expensive things are of little interest to me if the value is merely in so many diamonds or pearls". At the time they were made, the animals weren't very expensive. They'd have cost the equivalent of what you'd expect to pay for a good quality ornament today.'

'But they must be extremely valuable now?'

He nodded. 'And the day may come when they have to be sold to pay for a major repair such as the roof being replaced. But I hope that won't become necessary in Dad's time. For him, they're the milestones of his life with my mother. They were exceptionally close... the way married couples should be but seldom are.'

'Does that cynical tone mean you don't expect to emulate your parents?'

'I'd like to, but... who can say? We live in a different world with very different values. One in three marriages ends in divorce.'

'That's the negative view of statistics... the one always picked up by journalists and the prophets of doom on

TV. I prefer the positive view. Two out of three marriages last...four out of every six people choose the right partner.'

'Or make the best of a bad job,' was Adam's sardonic comment. He closed and re-locked the glass panels screening the alcove. 'If you take the optimist's view, why is it you're still single?'

'I was going to marry someone once,' Jane said quietly. 'He was killed in an accident.' She paused for a moment before asking, 'Why are you single?'

Instead of answering, he said, 'That must have been very tough. How old were you when it happened?'

'Eighteen.'

To her surprise he put an arm round her shoulders. 'Too young to cope with losing someone you love. It's hard enough at Dad's age.'

Coming on top of the way he had behaved earlier, his sympathy was disconcerting.

Without thinking, she said, 'But even worse at Dick's age. I was really too young to start a permanent relationship, and your father has had years of happiness. But poor Dick...losing a young wife and being left with a small boy...that must be really terrible.'

Adam withdrew his arm, but only to turn her to face him. 'I agree, but don't let your sympathy for him run away with you. You wouldn't be happy with him, you know.'

It was hard to interpret his expression. In spite of her earlier resolve not to reveal how things stood between her and Dick, she found herself saying, 'He thinks I would.'

Adam moved his hands, sliding the tips of his fingers behind her ears, caressing her cheeks with his thumbs and exploring the tender skin behind her lobes with his forefingers.

'He needs a woman in his life. Any good-tempered, capable girl who will mother his son and warm his slippers will do. Do you want a comfortable rut for the rest of your life?'

She wanted to say, Are you offering an alternative? but knew, if she did, his answer might dash all her hopes. He wanted her. That was obvious. But probably not the way she wished to be wanted—forever.

She played safe. 'Are you always so sure you know what's best for other people?'

'Not always. In this case, yes. Do you want me to prove it... again?'

His left hand slid to the base of her throat while his right plunged into her hair, cradling the back of her head so that there was no way to avoid the swoop of his mouth.

Not that she wanted to avoid it. He had already aroused her merely by touching her cheeks and the sensitive places behind her ears. The instant he started to kiss her she was back at the point she had reached while being kissed in the car; her insides melting, her heart beating like a tom-tom, her whole being burning with longing, silently begging to be taken.

And a moment later, feeling her lack of resistance, he slid his hands down her body, pressing her close, making her feel the power and urgency of his response.

Had they been alone in the house, there could only have been one end to it.

But they weren't, and a few moments later they heard his father's footsteps on the stretches of polished floor between the row of Persian and Turkish rugs carpeting the corridor.

Unhurriedly Adam released her. 'I have to leave here this evening to keep an early appointment in London tomorrow. I'll be back on Friday. Keep the evening free for me, will you?'

As his father re-entered the room, he said, 'I'm going to take Jane home now, Dad.'

'Oh, so soon?' Colonel Fontenay's disappointment seemed genuine. 'I was hoping to show her some more of your mother's treasures. You must come again soon, my dear.'

'I'll look forward to it...and thank you for letting me see all those lovely things,' she said, with a glance at the alcove.

'It was a pleasure. Thank you for the cake.'

Warmed by the kindness of his smile, she debated asking point-blank to be told his side of the story about the Fabergé cat, but decided this wasn't the moment.

But all the way home the Fontenays' failure to mention it fretted her, perhaps because very soon she would have to sidestep Hector's questions about how she had spent her day. It made her feel bad to deceive him. Although intellectually she knew it was nonsense, emotionally she had never quite been able to rid herself of the feeling that losing Nick had been her punishment for meeting him secretly and letting him make love to her.

Then, as if she hadn't learnt her lesson, she had fabricated a false persona for Adam, and now she was deceiving Hector. It wasn't right.

Glancing at Adam, she saw that he was frowning slightly and wondered what was on his mind.

On the outskirts of the village, he said, 'As I'm *person non grata* with your cousin, I'd better not drop you a your door.'

Jane braced herself to bring the issue into the open 'Why *are* you and your father on Hector's blacklist Adam? I'm sure you must realise how awkward it make things for me, yet you've never mentioned the subject I expected it to come up this afternoon, when we wer looking at your mother's collection, but neither of yo said a word.'

'What is there to say?' he answered. 'We aren't th only people the old man has his knife into. He's famou for his antipathies. I suppose, in our case, it's a forr of resentment because his business has declined an Dad's has prospered.'

'It's much more than that. Surely you can't imagin he sent you packing, the first time I came down to se him, merely because your father's done well and h hasn't?'

'Resentment and envy are powerful emotions,' sai Adam. 'They've been known to drive men to murder Now that you've cleaned his place up, it's easy to forge what a dump he had let it become. His outburst at m was probably prompted by an awareness of that... b his sense of failure.'

For the first time since she had known him, Jane wa suddenly conscious that basically he was a salesman, eve if that wasn't how Crowthorne's staff would describ themselves. His answer had been too smooth. Almos unctuous. And that wasn't like him. Somehow it didn' ring true.

She said, 'That wasn't the reason. What he's angr about is something far more specific. Surely yo know...surely you can't have forgotten why he dislikes you?'

'I shouldn't have thought it mattered much,' he said dismissively.

She had a strong impression that he wanted her to drop the subject.

'Well, in view of his fragile health, perhaps it doesn't,' she agreed. 'But if he weren't ill, it would. Anyway I'd have thought you'd want me to know your side of the story.'

'What has the old boy told you?'

'According to Hector, one of the Fabergé cats I saw this afternoon was virtually stolen from him.'

'How does he make that out?'

'He says one of his shop-minders sold it to you for two pounds fifty when it should have been two hundred and fifty...and that if you didn't know it was a mistake, your parents would have known at once.'

By now they had reached the village. Without commenting on her statement, Adam drove to a point midway along the goose beck, not far from but out of sight of Hector's shop window. There he parked and switched off the engine.

Turning to look directly at her, he said, 'And do you believe that?'

'No, I don't...but nor do I think that Hector is an outright liar. There has to be *some* truth in it. And the fact that you've accepted his animosity towards you without comment, and this afternoon made no reference to one of the cats having come from his shop—that does puzzle me. Why not explain what really happened?'

Adam took his time to reply. His glance shifted from her to a woman crossing the green with an elderly dog at her heels. He watched them for several moments before he said, 'I don't think there's anything to be gained by raking over the ashes of something that happened nearly twenty years ago. The breach between us and Hector isn't going to be repaired at this late date. Some of the facts you've been given are true and some aren't. There are times when one has to trust one's instinct, and that's what you'll have to do in this instance, Jane. I'll call you on Friday.'

He got out of the car and walked round to open the passenger door.

CHAPTER TEN

JANE found Hector asleep in a steamer chair in the small back garden she had reclaimed from the kangaroo vine and the nettles which had almost taken it over when she arrived.

There was still a lot of work to do before the garden was as pretty as some of its neighbours. But she had made a start, planting pelargoniums and sweet peas to give quick colour and scent. Aided by Ros Farnham, a generous donor of surplus cuttings and seedlings, Jane was aiming to make it a typical cottage garden where vegetables and herbs shared beds with Canterbury bells, hollyhocks and cornflowers.

But that would take time; and time, for Hector, was running out. He looked very frail lying in the old-fashioned chair with his carpet-slippered feet on the footrest and the awning shading his face.

In her absence he had had a visitor. There were two mugs beside the large brown teapot on a tray on the grass.

Quietly, so as not to disturb him, she took the tray indoors to wash the mugs and make a fresh pot of tea. She wondered who had been to see him. Apart from a few elderly dealers who turned up from time to time, he didn't have many friends. As Adam had said, he was renowned for his antipathies.

While waiting for the kettle to boil, she continued puzzling over the strangeness in Adam's manner when she had tried to get at the truth about the Fabergé cat. Suddenly it occurred to her that someone who might know the facts and be prepared to disclose them was Mrs Farnham. Ros had a foot in both camps; she was liked by and on good terms with the Fontenays and Hector.

'Jane... are you there?'

The call from the garden forced her to put aside thoughts of Adam and hurry outside.

'Yes, I'm back. Would you like some more tea?'

The old man glowered. 'No, I wouldn't. What's all this I hear about you going out with that young blackguard Fontenay?'

Her heart sank. Who had seen her with Adam and reported it to Hector?

Wondering how best to deal with the situation, she debated saying firmly that Adam wasn't a blackguard. The trouble was she still had no facts with which to rebut Hector's conviction that the Fontenays had robbed him.

'A fine way to repay all my kindness...letting yourself be bamboozled by that smooth-tongued rotter,' Hector said testily. 'I gave you credit for more sense. Especially when you've got a decent, honest chap like Dick Osborne offering to make an honest woman of you. He was round here this afternoon... wanting me to use my influence with you. What influence?' he said with sharp sarcasm. 'You don't give a damn for my opinion...any more than you cared for your father's.'

'Hector, that isn't fair,' she protested. 'Aunt Dee knew I was seeing Nick. She encouraged our friendship. And you're being unfair about Adam... he's not as black as you paint him. As a matter of fact I met him in London before I came here. I didn't set out to deceive you. I was just trying not to upset you.'

'So you say now you've been found out. People are always sorry when their misdeeds come to light. Are you on the Pill?' he shot at her.

'The Pill?' she said, taken aback. 'No... no, I'm not.'

'More fool you, then,' said Hector. 'Thought you'd have learned your lesson.'

Jane felt herself flushing scarlet. 'It doesn't arise.'

'What does that mean?'

'Adam and I aren't in that kind of relationship.'

'Not yet perhaps, but I've no doubt that's his objective. He'll never marry you, you know. The old man wouldn't allow it... wouldn't consider you good enough for his son and heir... especially not with your history. Have you told Osborne about that?'

She nodded. 'Dick knows about Apple, but——'

'And still wants to marry you. You should count yourself lucky. Even in these lax times, there aren't many men who want a girl with a child in tow.'

'Apple isn't in tow. I wish she were,' she said bitterly. 'That's the only thing I regret... not keeping her. *That* was my worst mistake. Not letting Nick make love to me... but forgetting to think about the possible consequences.'

'Well, I won't argue with that,' said Hector. 'We all do a few stupid things when we're growing up, and it wouldn't have turned out too badly if the child's father hadn't been killed. But now you're a full-grown woman who should have her head screwed on properly. You've no business seeing that fellow behind my back and playing fast and loose with Dick. You'll be safe with him... secure for the rest of your life. The best you can hope for from the other one is that, when he leaves you in the lurch, you won't be in the family way again.'

'There's no question of that,' said Jane. 'I'm not having an affair with Adam, only a friendship. As for Dick... I like him, but I don't love him. I never will.'

'Doesn't matter if you don't,' Hector said gruffly. 'Affection and trust... they're what counts. All this talk about falling in love is a lot of claptrap. Gives people a kick while it lasts... but how long is that? A few months, perhaps a year, and then it wears off and what's left? Disillusionment. Better by far to marry for sensible reasons. In your case a comfortable home and a reliable breadwinner, and in his case a capable woman to run his house and care for his son. Together you'd have other children. You wouldn't pine for Apple as much as you do now.'

When she didn't answer, he went on, 'You think I don't know what I'm talking about... that I'm too old to remember what it's like to be your age. You're wrong. I remember very clearly. Forty years ago I married for love and a fine hash the pair of us made of it. Cooing like doves at the start and before long spitting and snarling like cat and dog. Four years, it lasted. Trouble was, by the time we separated, the nice homely girl I should have picked had gone off with someone else. Made him a happy man too, from what I heard later. I never took the plunge again. Once bitten, twice shy, as they say.'

'I see. I've often wondered why you were a bachelor.'

'Now you know,' Hector said brusquely. 'So heed the voice of experience and don't make the same mistake. Dick isn't what used to be called a heart-throb. But he's steady and kind, and that's what counts in the long run.

Fontenay's son is a womaniser. He's more discreet now than he used to be, but I doubt if he's changed his ways. Once a rake, always a rake.'

'That's hearsay, Hector...not fact. Mrs Farnham speaks well of Adam.'

'Hmph...she speaks well of everyone...including her own useless husband,' the old man tartly. 'He was a well-known layabout, but to hear her talk you'd think he had been a saint. That good lady sees life through rose-coloured spectacles.'

'Perhaps that's the best way to see it,' Jane said drily. 'Better than always looking on the dark side.'

She wanted to ask what Dick had said about her relationship with Adam—how had he known she was out with Adam?—but was afraid of rekindling the old man's ire.

Later, when he was in bed, Dick rang up.

'I'm sorry if I put you on the spot this afternoon. The old boy thought you were out with me, didn't he?'

'He assumed that, yes. I didn't tell him I was meeting you. How did you know where I'd gone?'

'This isn't London, Jane. You can't keep things quiet in the country. Someone you met at our party spends Sunday mornings sailing. He told me he'd seen you when I went down to the pub for a pre-lunch beer. Did you enjoy yourself?'

'Yes, I did. We were a foursome. The surgeon who owns the boat, his girlfriend and Adam. Then I went back to tea at the Manor and was offered a job as assistant to Colonel Fontenay.'

'Are you going to take it?'

'Not while Hector needs me.'

'And afterwards?'

'I don't know, Dick... I'm not certain what I should do... afterwards.'

'I need you too,' he said, in a low voice. 'But I know I can't compete with Adam. According to my sister, he's every woman's dream. But she said that before he ditched her for someone else. Be careful with him, Jane. I'd hate you to be hurt the way Jill was.'

'I don't want you to be hurt either, Dick.'

'Is that an oblique way of saying that you're not going to marry me?'

Part of her wanted to say yes and end his uncertainty. Part of her was remembering what Hector had said a few hours earlier: 'Trouble was, by the time we separated, the nice homely girl I should have picked had gone off with someone else.'

Dick said quickly, 'You haven't made up your mind yet. Well, that's all right with me. Take as long as you like... months... a year. I can wait.'

Three nights later, between bedtime and sunrise, Hector Beccles died in his sleep.

Jane discovered he had gone when she took him an early cup of tea. Later she telephoned his doctor's private number and he called at the shop on his way to take morning surgery.

After signing the death certificate, he said kindly, 'Can you cope with the funeral arrangements? Would you like some help?'

'I can manage. Hector left instructions.'

Perhaps the doctor mentioned Hector's death to his nurse in the hearing of people in his waiting-room. By lunchtime the news was all round the village. Considering that Hector hadn't been universally popular, Jane was surprised by the number of people who called to offer condolences and assistance.

'That's partly because they like you, my dear,' said Ros Farnham, when she came to call about teatime. She had heard the news from the wife of Long Goosebeck's vicar. 'Look, I know you're a sensible girl, and he couldn't have lasted much longer. But it's always a shock when someone dies. You shouldn't be here on your own. Until the funeral is over, why not come and sleep at my house?'

'You are kind,' Jane said gratefully.

'Not at all. I'd be glad of your company. My place is far too large for a woman on her own. If I had any sense I'd sell it. But if I moved to a small house, the grandchildren wouldn't want to spend their holidays with me. It's the house they adore.'

'I'm sure they'd love staying with you wherever you lived,' Jane told her. 'You're a born home-maker. I recognised that the night I came to supper.'

Later, having her second meal in Mrs Farnham's cosy kitchen, she said, 'Ros...there's something on my mind. It's been fidgeting me since the first time I came to see Hector. I wish I could get to the bottom of it. I wonder if you know the truth?'

'The truth about what?'

'About the feud between Hector and the Fontenays.'

Mrs Farnham avoided her eyes. 'That breach was a long time ago. Don't you think it's better to let sleeping dogs lie?'

'No, I don't...not when someone's reputation is involved. Hector accused the Fontenays of doing him down. I can't believe they would stoop to shabby behaviour. Yet when I asked Adam about it, he was evasive.'

'Yes, he would be,' said Ros.

'Why?'

'It would go against Adam's code to damage, perhaps destroy your respect for Hector. He would rather you thought ill of him. Adam is his father's son, and Laurence Fontenay is a member of that endangered species, the true gentleman. A man whose word is his bond. A man who would rather die than behave dishonourably.'

After a pause to digest this, Jane said, 'So who *was* in the wrong? Hector?'

'I'm afraid so—yes. But what he did wasn't unusual. Most people in the trade would regard it as normal.'

'What did he do?'

'A woman came to his shop with some bits and pieces to sell. They had belonged to her granny, who had started her working life as a maid in a big house in Norfolk. In the way of dealers, Hector asked how much she wanted. She had no idea of their value and suggested two pounds for the lot. He said that was too much and offered her one pound fifty. Then he put the cat in the window, priced at two pounds fifty and the other things at similar mark-ups.'

'He told me the cat was marked two hundred and fifty and the price was misread by his shop-minder.'

Ros shook her head. 'Not true...although as time went on he came to believe it. Two hundred and fifty pounds was what a similar cat fetched in a London auction some years afterwards. The cat Adam gave his mother wouldn't have been worth as much as that when it passed through Mr Beccles' hands. But it would have been worth far more than he paid for it, and that bothered Laura Fontenay. She couldn't bear to think the seller hadn't received a fair price. So she made it her business to find out where it had come from...not too difficult in a rural community. Then Laura went to see her and gave her a better price.'

'Mrs Fontenay sounds a lovely person,' said Jane.

'She was...I still miss her very much,' Ros agreed, with a sigh. 'But unfortunately that generous impulse rebounded. The woman who sold the cat was a chatterbox. When the story spread to the ears of people who didn't like Hector, inevitably they passed it that he had cheated the seller.'

'Which, in a sense, he had,' said Jane.

'I wouldn't put it as strongly as that,' Ros said judicially. 'When it comes to buying and selling antiques, it's the seller who has to beware. They should make it their business to find out what objects are worth. It's not difficult. The public libraries are stuffed with books giving guidance.'

She paused before adding, 'Although it has to be said that at the time all this happened, only a select band of specialists knew much about Fabergé. Hector was an experienced dealer but he didn't recognise the Fabergé cat for what it was. The fact that he hadn't was an extra irritant when he heard that a schoolboy *had* recognised it. Later, reading in the paper about the price fetched by the other Fabergé cat exacerbated his annoyance. From then on he took agin the Fontenays and hadn't a good word to say for them.'

She rose from the table to clear their plates and serve the pudding.

Jane said, 'Last Sunday, when Hector found out I had been sailing with Adam, he was angry, but not as enraged as I would have expected him to be. I don't think he had the energy to lose his temper with me, poor old chap.'

'Probably not,' said Ros. 'And I shouldn't be surprised if these last months were some of the happiest of his life. We all need to feel loved and cared for. He never had that until you arrived to sort out the shambles he was living in. What are you going to do next, Jane? Or haven't you thought about it yet?'

'Not really. My god-daughter Apple is coming to stay very soon. I'll think about the future after she has gone home.'

The coach bringing Apple to Suffolk was due to arrive in Ipswich late in the afternoon. Having set out much too early, in a fever of impatience to be reunited with the child who meant so much to her, Jane arrived at the coach station with nearly an hour to wait.

But it wasn't only Apple who occupied her thoughts as she sat in the cafeteria, drinking coffee. The two men in her life were also on her mind.

She hadn't seen Adam since the Sunday he took her sailing. Notified by his father of Hector's death, he had telephoned from London to say the appropriate things and to cancel the tentative arrangement to meet the following Friday.

He hadn't been present at the funeral although Colonel Fontenay had been there, as had Dick and his father. Since then the colonel had telephoned more than once to enquire how she was and offer his assistance if she had any problems. But Adam had not been in touch

Jane had an uneasy feeling her demand for an explanation of Hector's dislike of the Fontenay's had offended him.

Or it might be that someone more attractive had entered his orbit in London and like many before her—if the rumours about him were true—she had been relegated to the ranks of Adam's past girlfriends.

Not that she had been his girlfriend in any but the most tenuous sense. Two dinner dates, four embraces, and a sailing foursome hardly constituted a serious relationship.

The coach from the North was on time but the first people to disembark were a party of pensioners who made slow work of alighting. But at last it was Apple's turn and she leapt down the steps and flung herself into Jane's arms with heart-warming eagerness.

'I'm longing to see where you live now,' she said excitedly, as they retrieved her small soft-topped suitcase from the coach's baggage hold.

'She's a sweet kid. Usually Tommy doesn't like girls, but he seems to have taken to her,' said Dick, one hot afternoon a week later.

He and Jane were sitting at the back of the beach, in the hollow of a sand dune. Near the sea's edge the two children were digging an elaborate network of channels for the tide, when it turned, to fill with water.

'I expect, having three brothers, she's more at ease with boys than some little girls,' Jane said lazily.

It was the second time since Apple's arrival that they had been to the coast with Dick and his son. Mr and Mrs Osborne had gone to the Lake District for a fortnight and, it being the slack season for auctioneers, Dick was taking a week of his annual holiday and might take another if the present heatwave continued.

As she lay back on her beach towel and closed her eyes against the bright light, Jane wondered if Dick's mother was as uneasy about what might be happening in her absence as she herself was about being here.

But Dick had made it difficult to refuse his invitations and it was good for Apple to mix with other children rather than being alone with Jane all the time. It would be dangerously easy to become too possessive with her.

'Sorry...what did you say?' She realised Dick had been speaking and she hadn't taken it in.

'Nothing important. You have a nap,' he said kindly.

Actually she wasn't sleepy, merely preoccupied. But if she pretended to doze it would prevent him from raising the subject of marriage. She knew it was on his mind, but she wasn't ready to talk about it again.

Dick had so much to offer, but whenever she thought about marrying him, a lean dark face with black eyebrows and an amorous mouth would appear in her mind's eye.

The night before last she had actually dreamed she was at her own wedding. When the officiating clergyman had asked if anyone knew of an impediment to the marriage, a strong voice had called out 'I do!' Then Adam had walked up the aisle to where she was standing at the chancel steps. But the man beside her hadn't been Dick. It had been Nick, her first love. There had been a time when she had dreamt of him often, and woken up weeping. But that was a long time ago.

They stayed at the beach until six, stopping on the way home to eat at a new pizza parlour.

'What about tomorrow?' said Dick, while the children, still hungry after large slices of pizza, were studying the illustrations on the shiny ice-cream menu.

'Tomorrow we're spending the day at Ros Farnham's place,' said Jane, uncomfortably aware of his disappointment.

Ros had invited some other children to lunch and prepared a picnic which they ate in the orchard while she and Jane and two mothers had more sophisticated fare at a table in the conservatory.

'Don't go yet,' she said to Jane, when the others were preparing to leave. 'If you've nothing better to do, stay for a leftovers supper.'

They were relaxing in the garden, with Apple lost in a book Ros had found for her, when they heard a car on the drive and the pip-pip of a horn.

'Oh, lord...who can this be?' said Ros. 'Trust someone to pop in for drinks the day I've run out of gin. No, sit tight——' as Jane made to rise from her lounger '—it may not be a social call.'

Less than a minute later, she reappeared. But not alone. Adam was with her.

'A visitor who brings his own liquor supply is always welcome,' said Ros, flourishing a paper-wrapped bottle. 'I'll fix you an iced Bulldog, Adam.'

She went back into the house.

'Hello, Jane. How are you?'

Adam sat down on a green-painted Victorian cast-iron garden chair for which Ros had made a green and white ticking cushion.

'I'm fine, thanks. And you?'

'Better now I'm out of London...not the best place to be in this scorching weather.'

Judging by his clothes, he had come straight from the city and not yet been to the Manor. He had left the jacket of his city suit in the car, and discarded the formal tie that, earlier today, he would have been wearing with his striped poplin shirt. Now this had its collar unbuttoned and its sleeves rolled halfway up his forearms. He had also discarded his city shoes and socks and was wearing a pair of blue Topsiders.

Following her glance at his bare brown ankles, he said, 'If I'd had some shorts with me, I'd have got rid of these too...' indicating his trousers. 'You look very cool and relaxed.'

She was cool, but had stopped being relaxed from the moment she saw who Ros's visitor was.

'I've had a lazy day. Ros asked us to lunch and we're staying to eat up the leftovers.'

'We?'

'I have my god-daughter staying with me. She's deep in a book somewhere down in the orchard.'

'I see.' He stretched his long legs, crossing them at the ankle. 'How long is she here for?'

'Two weeks...possibly longer. Her brothers are at a boys' summer camp. It gives my sister and her husband some time to themselves.'

Ros reappeared with a tray bearing three tall glasses. 'As you're both driving, I haven't made these very strong.' She offered the tray to Jane. 'Bulldogs were my husband's favourite summer evening drink.'

'What's in them?'

'Gin and the juice of an orange topped up with chilled ginger ale. Don't worry. Not much gin.'

'*Skol!*' Adam raised his glass to them before tasting its amber contents. 'Mmm . . . wonderful stuff at the end of a long, hot drive.'

'You haven't been around for a while,' said Ros.

'It's been a busy time,' he told her. 'I've been supervising arrangements for a major sale in the autumn, the BBC have been making a film about how Crowthorne's functions and on top of that I've been asked to write a book about lost and found masterpieces.'

'How exciting! Are you going to do it?'

'Probably. It's surprising how many pictures have turned up in odd places. One of Lord Leighton's finest paintings spent forty years in the men's room of a deserted building in Connecticut, and a very beautiful drawing by Gainsborough was lost for sixty years because its owner died in the sinking of the Titanic.'

'When is the film about Crowthorne's going to be televised?' asked Jane.

'Not for some time. They spent several days disrupting my department, but it wouldn't surprise me if most of what they shot is cut.'

Apple came into view, pausing uncertainly when she saw an unknown man with them. Ros smiled and beckoned, telling Adam who she was and, when Apple reached the terrace, introducing him to her.

The child held out her hand. 'How do you do?' she said politely.

His response was equally formal. Taking the small hand in his, he said gravely, 'How do you do?' Then he smiled at her. 'We're having cold drinks called Bulldogs. Would you like one?'

'Yes, please.'

When Ros would have risen, he stayed her with a gesture. 'Sit tight...I'll get it.'

Jane shifted her position on the lounger to make room for Apple to sit beside her. For some reason the sight of her daughter's small paw being engulfed by Adam's powerful hand had brought a lump to her throat. She knew it had been a moment she would remember forever: the first meeting of the two people she loved best in the world, neither of whom knew how much they meant to her.

'Adam often drops in to say hello on his way home from London,' said Ros. 'I call him my honorary son and in many ways he's more thoughtful than my real sons. They *sometimes* remember to replenish their old mum's drinks cupboard, but more often they deplete it. You can bet he'll have something in the car for his father as well. If not a bottle, a book, or a goodie from that marvellous delicatessen in Soho.'

He came back with the drink for Apple. 'I left out the gin which I didn't think you would like,' he told her, with the smile which had been conspicuously missing from his exchanges with Jane.

Apple grinned. 'Why are they called Bulldogs?'

'You'd have to ask whoever invented it. Drinks are often named after animals...Mule's Hind Leg, Prairie Chicken, Barking Dog, Silver Stallion.'

Instead of sitting down, he said, 'I've been sitting in a car since half-past three. I need a wander round the garden. Like to come with me?'

Apple nodded then glanced at Jane who said, 'Go ahead.'

'He's good with children,' Ros said, when they were out of earshot. 'I wish he'd hurry up and get married.'

'Perhaps he doesn't need to,' said Jane. 'I shouldn't think lonely nights are one of his problems.'

'Probably not...in his salad days. But if you've heard gossip about him, don't believe all of it. A lot of the stories are long out of date. He once told me he wanted what his parents had...an enduring partnership.'

When, ten minutes later, Adam and Apple reappeared, she was holding his hand. Jane was surprised the child had taken to him so quickly, until she remembered how rapidly she herself had succumbed to his charm at their first meeting.

She watched them strolling across the grass, his dark head bent as he listened to whatever the little girl was telling him. She wondered if Ros would ask him to stay to supper and found herself praying that she would.

But when they got back to the terrace, Adam said, 'I must be off. I told Dad I'd be back by seven and it's six-thirty now. Don't bother to see me out, Ros.'

Putting his hands on the arms of her lounger, he bent to kiss her cheek. 'Bye-bye, Apple. Cheerio, Jane.'

Apple was chucked under the chin. His farewell to Jane was an enigmatic nod.

On the way home, Apple said, 'Adam told me about someone else called Apple.'

'Did he say you could call him Adam?'

'Yes. He said Mr Fauntleroy was too much of a mouthful.'

'His surname isn't Fauntleroy, love.' *Little Lord Fauntleroy* was one of the Victorian books Mrs Chichester had given Jane to send to Apple. 'It's Fontenay. Who is this other Apple?'

'She was the King of Bohemia's daughter. He wasn't really a king but that's what everyone called him. He was married to an American lady who collected paintings. Peggy Googlysomething.'

'Peggy Guggenheim?'

'Yes, that's it. How did you know?'

'Both she and her collection of paintings were very famous... still are. But I didn't know about the King of Bohemia and his daughter called Apple. How interesting.'

'Adam is very interesting,' Apple said seriously. 'I liked him. Didn't you?'

'I've met him before... and his father. They're both nice,' Jane answered casually.

Later that evening, when Apple was asleep, she had a bath and then put on a clean pair of jeans and a fresh T-shirt to sit outside while the long late summer dusk deepened into darkness.

For a while, comfortably stretched in Hector's steamer chair, she thought about him and Olivia Chichester and how much she owed to them both. Now she had everything she had dreamed of: a little house, a garden, a nest egg, the promise of a job or, if she were prepared to take the risk, a business she might be able to keep going.

So, when she ought to be counting her blessings and feeling extremely contented, especially with Apple staying here, why did she feel like crying?

The sound of the doorbell forced her to pull herself together. She hoped it was only one of her neighbours who was calling on her. If it were Dick, she would have to break it to him that she could never marry for practical reasons, not while her heart was yearning for someone else.

But it wasn't Dick. When she released the door-blind to see who was outside, it was Adam's tall figure she saw.

She stared at him in astonished silence until he mouthed, 'May I come in?'

Quickly she unlocked the door, stepping back to admit him.

'Is Apple in bed?' he asked.

'Yes.'

'Good. I want to talk to you...but not in her presence.'

Jane pulled down the blind, locked the door and led the way to the back room.

'Will you have a cup of coffee?'

'No, thanks. I've just had some. We were late having dinner tonight.'

'Have you come to tell me that the job with your father is no longer open?'

'On the contrary, he's as keen as ever to have you as his assistant. He was talking about it tonight. But he doesn't want to press you. The reason I'm here is...personal.'

'Personal?' she said uncertainly.

'Apple is your child, isn't she?'

She was taken aback. 'What makes you say that?'

'The way you look at her. The likeness between you. Not a striking physical resemblance...something more subtle...yet obvious to anyone who's watched you as closely as I have. If I'm right, it explains all the things about you which don't make sense.'

'What sort of things?'

'Chiefly the fact that you're on your own. There has to be some special reason for that...something more than the loss of the boy you loved at eighteen.'

'Thousands of women are on their own.'

Although she had gestured for him to sit down, he was still on his feet, as she was. Suddenly he moved closer, taking her by the shoulders.

'Not when they're as lovely...as lovable as you are.'

He looked down into her startled eyes, and all at once his expression, usually so enigmatic, was like a face stripped of a mask.

Gone was the courteous indifference of his manner towards her this afternoon. Gone was the self-control he had only once allowed to slip.

But this time it wasn't anger she saw in his eyes. All her own feelings were mirrored there.

'You must know I love you,' he said huskily. 'Everyone else does. I want to marry you, Jane. I want to spend the rest of my life looking after you...making you happy. I would have told you before, but every time we seemed to be making progress you pulled back...retreated from me. Until today I couldn't understand it. I thought perhaps I was wrong...that you didn't love me. Now, after meeting Apple, I think it's because you've been hurt. You're afraid of love...afraid of being wounded again...'

He pulled her close to him, wrapping both arms tightly round her. She could feel his heart beating, feel him shaking with repressed emotion.

He spoke hoarsely into her hair. 'Trust me, Jane...trust your instincts. We belong together. You can't marry Dick. I won't let you. It would be crazy. You're mine...you've always been mine.'

She struggled to free herself, but only until he loosened his hold enough to let her slip her arms round his neck. Her face alight with relief and joy, she said, 'I know that...but I didn't know you felt the same way. I thought you might just be...scalp-hunting. And even if you were serious, I thought you'd change your mind when you knew about my past.'

'It's our future that matters, not our pasts. Did you seriously think me such a self-righteous prig that knowing about Apple would change my feelings about you?'

'I hoped not...I wasn't sure. The double standard still exists. Your father won't like it when he knows.'

'Dad adores you. It may surprise him, but it won't make a jot of difference to the way he feels about you.'

'I hope not. Oh, Adam...kiss me.'

It was wonderful to surrender her lips to his without any need to hold back, without any doubts about his motives. As she yielded to his strong arms and passionate kisses, it was hard to believe that only a little while ago she had been in despair, convinced that this could never happen.

Presently, loosening his hold, he said thickly, 'I wish I could stay...or take you back to my place. But having waited so long, I guess I can wait a little longer.' He put her gently away from him. 'Perhaps you'd better make that coffee you mentioned.'

Her senses on fire, her whole body aching for love, Jane did as he suggested. A few moments later, standing in the kitchen doorway, Adam said, 'How soon can we be married? A special licence is the quickest way, I believe.'

'Is it? I don't really know.'

'Apple could be your bridesmaid. She'd like that, wouldn't she? Most little girls like dressing up.'

'I'm sure she'd love it.'

'She told me quite a lot about herself. I gather she lives with your sister...calls her Mummy.'

'Yes, she doesn't know about me.'

'How did that come about?'

Waiting for the kettle to boil, Jane began to tell him all the things he didn't yet know about her.

The following morning Adam rang up to say he had told his father their news.

'He couldn't be more delighted, darling.'

'Have you told him everything?'

'Everything. He wants you both to come to lunch, by which time I'll have fixed up some leave of absence and organised a licence. Listen, before we tell anyone else, I think you should tell Dick Osborne how things stand between us. Now that you're promised to me, I feel more sympathetic towards him.'

'I'll go and see him this morning,' Jane promised. 'I must do it face to face.'

In fact Jane had been thinking about breaking the news to Dick ever since she got up. It had been after midnight when Adam left her and by then she had been too keyed-up, too happy, to fall asleep quickly. But in spite of only five hours' sleep, she didn't feel tired. If it hadn't been for the painful interview ahead of her, she could have truthfully said she had never felt better.

'How did it go?' Adam asked, when she arrived at the Manor at a quarter to one.

'As you'd expect, knowing Dick. He did his best to make light of it, but I feel terrible for ever letting him think it a possibility.'

He put his arm round her shoulders. 'If anyone's to blame, it's me for not chancing my arm a lot sooner. But don't worry too much about him. There'll be someone else for Dick. He's a nice guy. Things will go right for him.'

'I hope so. I'm very fond of him.'

'I know. That's what had me worried,' Adam said drily. 'From an onlooker's point of view, it can be hard to distinguish between affection and love.'

After lunch, Colonel Fontenay said, 'Take Apple up to your flat and show her your fairground horses, Adam. I want a word with Jane.'

She felt a twinge of apprehension. Now that he'd had time to assimilate his son's announcement, was the colonel having misgivings? Rather than airing them to Adam, was he going to tackle her?

Yet his welcome, when she arrived, had seemed both warm and sincere. She had felt he was genuinely glad about their engagement, and the fact that she had a child made no difference to him.

After Adam and Apple had left the room, the older man said, 'When my son broke his news at breakfast, it came as no surprise. Do you remember the day he introduced us at the view of the admiral's sale?'

'Of course.'

'I knew then that you had to be the mysterious girl he had fallen in love with at that exhibition of paintings of beautiful women. That was the night of my break-in. Adam came home in the small hours, bursting with excitement. As soon as he was satisfied that I hadn't been seriously hurt, he came out with it. "Dad, I've met the most glorious girl. I'm going to marry her".'

The colonel paused to smile at her, relieving Jane of any lingering anxiety that he had any reservations about Adam's choice of a wife.

'But then something went wrong,' he continued. 'The poor fellow was like a bear with a sore head for months. I didn't probe. No point. He obviously didn't want to discuss it. Then you reappeared and I knew that whatever had gone wrong between you would soon be put right.'

'I wish I had shared your confidence,' Jane said, with a rueful smile.

Presently, when Adam brought Apple downstairs, the colonel beckoned her to him.

'People who are newly engaged have a great deal to talk about. I've been invited to tea with a friend who has a swimming-pool. Would you like to come with me so that Jane and Adam can plan their wedding in peace?'

'Yes, please,' said Apple. Then her forehead furrowed. 'But I haven't got my bathing suit with me.'

'That's not a problem. Mrs Morris has a flock of grandchildren. She's sure to have one to fit you, and a snorkel and flippers as well, I shouldn't wonder.'

'Very tactful,' said Adam, when his father and Apple had gone and they were alone. 'I've been wondering how to get you to myself. Come here.' He opened his arms.

Jane needed no second bidding. She had been longing to be alone with him. With Apple around they were almost as rigorously chaperoned as a Victorian courting couple. But now, thanks to his father, they had at least two hours' respite from the unwitting restraints imposed by their small duenna.

The housekeeper's room on the top floor received the afternoon sun. With the window open, the scent of sweet peas drifted up from the garden below in delicate, elusive gusts. From time to time there was a flurry of wings as a dozen white doves flew past, circling the house before returning to base on the stable roof where they spent their days preening and strutting.

The sun burnished Adam's tanned shoulders as Jane lay on his tumbled bed in the lazy aftermath of love. He was leaning over her, smiling, his eyes possessive and tender.

'What time is it? Ought we to dress?' she murmured, reluctant to come down to earth.

'There's no hurry. They won't be back yet. Are you happy?'

She reached up to touch his dark hair. 'Unbelievably, impossibly happy. You can't imagine how happy.'

'Don't be silly,' he said gently. 'It's the same for me. And this is just the beginning, the overture. Listen, darling, I think as soon as we're married we should take Apple back to your sister and try to straighten things out. She has to know the truth some time.' His voice deepened as he went on, 'You've had your share of unhappiness. From now on it's going to be different.'

Jane's eyes gleamed with tears, but they were tears of joy. 'It already is,' she whispered, and drew his head down to hers.

INDULGE A LITTLE 6947 SWEEPSTAKES
NO PURCHASE NECESSARY

HERE'S HOW THE SWEEPSTAKES WORKS:
The Harlequin Reader Service shipments for January, February and March 1994 will contain, respectively, coupons for entry into three prize drawings: a trip for two to San Francisco, an Alaskan cruise for two and a trip for two to Hawaii. To be eligible for any drawing using an Entry Coupon, simply complete and mail according to directions.

There is no obligation to continue as a Reader Service subscriber to enter and be eligible for any prize drawing. You may also enter any drawing by hand printing your name and address on a 3" x 5" card and the destination of the prize you wish that entry to be considered for (i.e., San Francisco trip, Alaskan cruise or Hawaiian trip). Send your 3" x 5" entries to: Indulge a Little 6947 Sweepstakes, c/o Prize Destination you wish that entry to be considered for, P.O. Box 1315, Buffalo, NY 14269-1315, U.S.A. or Indulge a Little 6947 Sweepstakes, P.O. Box 610, Fort Erie, Ontario L2A 5X3, Canada.

To be eligible for the San Francisco trip, entries must be received by 4/30/94; for the Alaskan cruise, 5/31/94; and the Hawaiian trip, 6/30/94. No responsibility is assumed for lost, late or misdirected mail. Sweepstakes open to residents of the U.S. (except Puerto Rico) and Canada, 18 years of age or older. All applicable laws and regulations apply. Sweepstakes void wherever prohibited.

For a copy of the Official Rules, send a self-addressed, stamped envelope (WA residents need not affix return postage) to: Indulge a Little 6947 Rules, P.O. Box 4631, Blair, NE 68009, U.S.A.

INDR93

INDULGE A LITTLE 6947 SWEEPSTAKES
NO PURCHASE NECESSARY

HERE'S HOW THE SWEEPSTAKES WORKS:
The Harlequin Reader Service shipments for January, February and March 1994 will contain, respectively, coupons for entry into three prize drawings: a trip for two to San Francisco, an Alaskan cruise for two and a trip for two to Hawaii. To be eligible for any drawing using an Entry Coupon, simply complete and mail according to directions.

There is no obligation to continue as a Reader Service subscriber to enter and be eligible for any prize drawing. You may also enter any drawing by hand printing your name and address on a 3" x 5" card and the destination of the prize you wish that entry to be considered for (i.e., San Francisco trip, Alaskan cruise or Hawaiian trip). Send your 3" x 5" entries to: Indulge a Little 6947 Sweepstakes, c/o Prize Destination you wish that entry to be considered for, P.O. Box 1315, Buffalo, NY 14269-1315, U.S.A. or Indulge a Little 6947 Sweepstakes, P.O. Box 610, Fort Erie, Ontario L2A 5X3, Canada.

To be eligible for the San Francisco trip, entries must be received by 4/30/94; for the Alaskan cruise, 5/31/94; and the Hawaiian trip, 6/30/94. No responsibility is assumed for lost, late or misdirected mail. Sweepstakes open to residents of the U.S. (except Puerto Rico) and Canada, 18 years of age or older. All applicable laws and regulations apply. Sweepstakes void wherever prohibited.

For a copy of the Official Rules, send a self-addressed, stamped envelope (WA residents need not affix return postage) to: Indulge a Little 6947 Rules, P.O. Box 4631, Blair, NE 68009, U.S.A.

INDR93

INDULGE A LITTLE
SWEEPSTAKES

OFFICIAL ENTRY COUPON

This entry must be received by: MAY 31, 1994
This month's winner will be notified by: JUNE 15, 1994
Trip must be taken between: JULY 31, 1994-JULY 31, 1995

YES, I want to win the Alaskan Cruise vacation for two. I understand that the prize includes round-trip airfare, one-week cruise including private cabin, all meals and pocket money as revealed on the "wallet" scratch-off card.

Name ______________________________

Address ____________________ Apt. ____________

City ______________________________

State/Prov. ______________ Zip/Postal Code ______________

Daytime phone number ______________________________
(Area Code)

Account # ______________________________

Return entries with invoice in envelope provided. Each book in this shipment has two entry coupons—and the more coupons you enter, the better your chances of winning!

 MONTH2

INDULGE A LITTLE
SWEEPSTAKES

OFFICIAL ENTRY COUPON

This entry must be received by: MAY 31, 1994
This month's winner will be notified by: JUNE 15, 1994
Trip must be taken between: JULY 31, 1994-JULY 31, 1995

YES, I want to win the Alaskan Cruise vacation for two. I understand that the prize includes round-trip airfare, one-week cruise including private cabin, all meals and pocket money as revealed on the "wallet" scratch-off card.

Name ______________________________

Address ____________________ Apt. ____________

City ______________________________

State/Prov. ______________ Zip/Postal Code ______________

Daytime phone number ______________________________
(Area Code)

Account # ______________________________

Return entries with invoice in envelope provided. Each book in this shipment has two entry coupons—and the more coupons you enter, the better your chances of winning!

© 1993 HARLEQUIN ENTERPRISES LTD. MONTH2